"You can let me go now."

"What if I don't want to?"

Oh, God! He was going to kiss her. Bad idea. Really bad. For so many reasons.

She placed her hands on his arms and gave a gentle push. "Chase, you can't."

"Can't what? Walk you to your truck?"

If Jolyn's knee didn't still hurt like the dickens, she'd kick herself. He wasn't going to kiss her. And she couldn't feel like a bigger fool.

"Or do you mean this?" he asked and turned her fear—or was it her secret hope?—into a reality.

Chase's lips sought hers, settled into place and very quickly took control. Her reluctance lasted a mere two seconds before she succumbed with a sigh that slipped out of its own volition.

Much, much better than any painkiller.

Dear Reader,

I enjoy writing about heroines who work in jobs more frequently held by men. After twenty years as the owner of a commercial construction company, I can relate to that. Up until now, however, I've never applied my personal experience to a book. Jolyn Sutherland in *The Family Plan* is the owner of a fledgling construction company and is a character close to my heart. Not only because she faces the normal challenges of running her own business, one where she competes against established men, but also because she must overcome a physical limitation, the result of a terrible accident the previous year. I guess one could say that *The Family Plan* is a book of role reversals. The hero, Chase Raintree, is a single parent with sole custody of his eight-year-old daughter. He's a great dad, but just like any single mother, has trouble balancing his job as a large-animal veterinarian— the only one in town—with being a parent. Everyday trials and tribulations, watching the characters struggle with and eventually overcome them, is what makes a book resonate with me. I hope you enjoy reading *The Family Plan* and that Jolyn and Chase's story resonates with you in some way, too.

Warmest wishes,

Cathy McDavid

P.S. I love hearing from readers. Visit my Web site at www.cathymcdavid.com to drop me a line.

The Family Plan
CATHY McDAVID

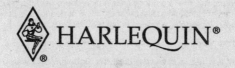

HARLEQUIN®

TORONTO • NEW YORK • LONDON
AMSTERDAM • PARIS • SYDNEY • HAMBURG
STOCKHOLM • ATHENS • TOKYO • MILAN • MADRID
PRAGUE • WARSAW • BUDAPEST • AUCKLAND

ISBN-13: 978-0-373-75201-0
ISBN-10:   0-373-75201-6

THE FAMILY PLAN

Printed in U.S.A.

ABOUT THE AUTHOR

For the past eleven years Cathy McDavid has been juggling a family, a job and writing and doing pretty well at it except for the cooking and housecleaning part. Mother of boy and girl teenage twins, she manages the near impossible by working every day with her husband of twenty years at their commercial construction company. They survive by not bringing work home and not bringing home to the office. A mutual love of all things Western also helps. Horses and ranch animals have been a part of Cathy's life since she moved to Arizona as a child and asked her mother for riding lessons. She can hardly remember a time when she couldn't walk outside and pet a soft, velvety nose (or beak, or snout) whenever the mood struck.

To my mother, who has always shown me by example just what I'm capable of accomplishing.

Chapter One

Jolyn Sutherland swung open the rear door of her horse trailer, retreated a safe distance and waited for the explosion. It came right on schedule.

Sinbad, her seventeen-year-old paint gelding, charged backward out of the trailer, legs thrashing, hooves clattering and sides heaving. He came to stop only when all four feet were firmly planted on the ground—for about two seconds. Jolyn grabbed his dangling lead rope before he trotted off in search of the barn and the barrel of oats he knew was waiting for him.

"That old horse never did trailer worth a lick."

Jolyn looked up to see a familiar face. "Dad!"

"You made it." Milt Sutherland strode toward her. "How was the drive down the mountain?"

"Touch and go in one or two spots. But we managed." Ignoring the ribbons of pain that shot up her right leg, she rushed to meet him, a whinnying Sinbad in tow.

Her father enveloped her in a bear hug and for a brief moment, Jolyn was a little girl again, her big, strong Daddy making everything all right. "It's good to be home," she said, her face buried in his shirtfront.

"It's good to have you home, sweetie pie."

She'd missed Blue Ridge, missed living in a town where folks waved when they drove past and karaoke night at Sage's

Bar and Grill was considered big entertainment. The only thing better than watching the morning sun peek slowly over the top of Saddle Horn Butte was watching the evening sun set in the distant Verde Mountains.

Jolyn loved touring and wouldn't have traded the last nine years on the road for anything except this, her father's arms holding her tight.

"Your mother's in the kitchen," he said, "fixing enough food to feed an army. She's been a nervous wreck the last few days, worried sick you wouldn't survive the drive from Dallas in one piece. Especially in this heat. I swear summer comes earlier every year."

Jolyn thought it was probably just the opposite. Her dad, not her mom, had been the nervous wreck.

"Well, we're here." She drew back after giving him a smacking kiss on the cheek. "Safe and sound."

"Safe, yes. Don't know about the sound part."

"What do you mean?"

Her dad nodded pointedly in Sinbad's direction.

She spun around and let out a gasp. "Oh, my gosh! How did that happen?" Bending over, she inspected Sinbad's left side.

The horse sported a nasty gash just behind his shoulder. The wound, in the shape of a jagged V, was at least four inches long and deep from the looks of it. Blood had seeped out, staining the horse's hide a dark red.

"I checked the trailer this morning in Phoenix before we loaded him," she said, her voice echoing her dismay. "So did Uncle Leroy."

Jolyn had stayed with various friends and relatives on her four-day trip cross-country from Texas to Arizona's north country, including stopping to have lunch today with her brother in Pineville. She'd taken her time traveling, not wanting to wear Sinbad—or herself—out.

Her father came to stand beside her, the two of them contemplating the horse's injury. "He must have run up on something between Pineville and here. The gate maybe."

"I suppose." Jolyn straightened and shook her head. The mountain road did twist and turn, but she'd driven slowly. Five miles under the posted speed limit the entire way.

"That horse has always been clumsy."

She swallowed the retort on the tip of her tongue. It was easier for some people to blame the horse rather than the rider. Jolyn knew better. She, and not Sinbad, was at fault for each of their mishaps, including the last. This latest one was no exception.

"He's excitable. That's what made him a champion barrel racer and headlining performer."

Her father smiled. "He was good in his day. So were you."

At twenty years old, Jolyn had left Blue Ridge and joined the Wild and Wooly West Equestrian Show. She and Sinbad traveled with the show until fourteen months ago, their signature bareback jump over a wagon full of mock settlers one of the show's biggest crowd pleasers.

In a split second, the time it took for Sinbad's right rear hoof to catch on the side of the wagon, their career was cut short. Sinbad was laid up for six weeks after the accident. Jolyn for six months. She was lucky she could walk again, much less drive a truck and trailer.

It was the worst and, if things went well for her here in Blue Ridge, the best thing to ever happen to her.

"Do you have any antibiotics in the barn?" she asked her dad while patting Sinbad's neck.

"No. My supplies are a little low."

She wasn't surprised. Her parents hadn't kept horses on the property since she moved out. Anything out in the barn had been recently purchased in anticipation of her coming home.

She reached for her cell phone in her pocket. "I'm going to call Chase."

"Is that really necessary? He's probably in the middle of dinner."

"It's a bad cut, Dad, and needs to be treated."

"We've got some peroxide in the house."

"I'd feel better if Chase looked at it."

Chase Raintree was the local veterinarian, the only one in a thirty-five-mile radius. He and Jolyn had been friends since before they could remember. Despite only sporadic contact in recent years, she was certain he'd come if she asked him— in the middle of dinner or not.

"The horse'll be fine until morning," her father said, dismissing her concerns. "You can head over to the feed store first thing after breakfast and pick up some medicine."

"I will if Chase isn't available."

She flipped open her cell phone and began to press buttons, assuming the number hadn't changed. Chase had taken over his parents' house when they semiretired and moved to Mesa a few years earlier and lived there with his eight-year-old daughter, Mandy.

Jolyn's father stayed her hand. "Maybe that's not such a good idea."

"Why?" She gave him a curious stare.

"Your mother and he are…well, let's just say they're having a difference of opinion."

"About Mandy?" Jolyn asked.

"Yeah."

"Oh, no." Jolyn's heart sank. "I thought Mom agreed to let that go."

"She's recently changed her mind."

"Why didn't you tell me?"

Her father heaved a tired sigh. "I didn't want to upset you before your trip. Figured you had enough to deal with."

Jolyn groaned. "What brought this on?"

"I'm not sure. Mandy started taking lessons…oh, sometime last fall I guess it was. But your mother didn't get pushy with Chase again until recently."

Dottie Sutherland operated a small dance studio out of the community center, offering classes three afternoons a week and Saturday mornings. Most of the girls in town, and even the occasional boy, studied under her at one point or another while growing up. As a child, Jolyn endured two years of lessons before permanently trading her tap shoes for cowboy boots.

"Can't you stop her?" Jolyn asked.

Her father raised one eyebrow and gave a short laugh. "You're joking, of course."

She hadn't been but didn't contradict him.

"This isn't just about Mom. There are other people's feelings to consider, including Mandy's. She still doesn't know, does she?"

"I don't think so."

"I can't support Mom in this if it means hurting Mandy." *Or going against Chase,* she added silently.

Her father scowled. "I don't know what's with your mother lately. She's been acting funny."

"Funny how?"

"Just not her usual self." He exhaled. "I've asked her again and again what's wrong but she keeps insisting nothing's the matter."

"Maybe I can get her to open up."

"It's worth a shot, I guess." His tone implied she'd get no further with her mother than he had.

Sinbad, evidently tired of standing in one place, began pawing the ground. The movement caused his injury to gape and seep fresh blood.

Jolyn made a decision. As much as she wanted to see her mother and get to the bottom of whatever was bothering her, Sinbad's injury needed attending. Turning him around, she walked toward the trailer. "I'm going to drive over to Chase's." She hated loading the horse back into the trailer after a grueling four-day road trip but saw no other choice.

Her father followed her. "What about supper? Your mother won't be happy after all the work she's put into it."

"This won't take long."

"You baby that horse too much considering what he did to you."

"Not now, Dad. Please." She'd just returned home after a long absence and wasn't in the mood to dredge up old arguments. To ease the tension, she gave him another kiss on the cheek. "I won't be long, I promise."

Chase lived half a mile away. She'd phone him on the drive over there. If he happened to be away, she'd wait for him and cleanse Sinbad's wound using a garden hose.

And what if he doesn't want to see you?

Of course he does, Jolyn told herself. Chase might be angry with her mother but he'd never refuse to treat a sick or injured animal.

He'd looked good the last time she'd seen him—two Christmases ago, was it?—though tired. His dark brown eyes had lacked their usual warmth, and his killer smile struck her as forced. The divorce and grueling custody battle had obviously taken a toll on him. Had he changed since then? And what would he think about the changes in her? Both the good and bad ones? Would he even notice?

It occurred to Jolyn that her need to rush Sinbad over to Chase's house might be motivated by her desire to see him, especially now that he was single again.

Before loading Sinbad she inspected the inside of the trailer. Finding no sharp edge on the gate that might have caused the cut, she erred on the side of caution and chose to put him on the left side of the gate this time. The big paint initially balked at going back into the trailer but finally complied after much coaxing. Jolyn shut the door behind him and dropped the latch in place.

Her father rested a hand on her shoulder. "This isn't all your mother's fault. You can't blame her entirely."

"No, it's not all her fault."

It was her brother Steven's fault when, nine years ago, he'd decided to have an affair with SherryAnne, Jolyn's one-time best friend and Chase's wife of three months. To this day, no one knew for certain who Mandy's biological father was. Not even SherryAnne, at least as far as she was telling.

CHASE WALKED OUT of the house, the screen door banging shut behind him. He spotted Jolyn's truck pulling into his driveway, and a smile tugged at the corners of his mouth. She'd returned to Blue Ridge. Hopefully, to stay. He hadn't realized until now how much he missed her.

When she approached, he motioned her on, signaling she should park near the barn, next to his truck. She gave him a wave as she rolled past. Chase followed, hurrying his steps. He rounded the back end of the trailer at the same moment she hopped out of the truck cab.

"Hey there." She came toward him, grinning from ear to ear.

He avoided staring at her pronounced limp and kept his eyes focused on her face. It wasn't exactly a hardship. Jolyn had always been a cute girl. She'd grown up into a very attractive woman. Hell, she'd just plain grown up. Chase didn't recall her filling out a T-shirt quite that nicely.

"Hey there, yourself." He scooped her up in an impulsive hug and swung her around in a circle. She felt nice in his arms. So nice, he didn't let her go right away. "It's good to see you again, Beanie."

She pulled out of his embrace and glared at him with enough heat to blister paint. "I'm leaving right this minute and never coming back if you call me that awful name one more time."

"String Bean Sutherland," he teased.

"You're as bad as you ever were."

"Some say I'm worse."

Her voice dropped in pitch. "Do tell."

Was she flirting with him? Or, more precisely, flirting back? The Jolyn he remembered was too shy, too serious, too self-conscious around men to engage in lighthearted sexual banter. What, besides nearly losing her right leg, had happened to her during the last nine years?

She looked the same. Well, almost the same. Her brown hair sported blond highlights and was cut in a shorter, more sophisticated style. She'd also taken to wearing makeup. Not much, just enough to enhance her hazel eyes and full mouth. Dallas had obviously agreed with Jolyn. He liked the new her, liked seeing her finally come into her own.

Easy, boy. Chase took a mental step back, reminding himself this wasn't just Jolyn, one of his oldest and closest friends. This was Dottie Sutherland's daughter, and Dottie was a woman dead set on making his life miserable. No, ruining it.

About the same time Chase sobered, a loud bang came from inside her horse trailer. Sinbad was making his displeasure known.

Jolyn shook her head. "I'd better get him out before he kicks a hole in the door."

"So, what scrape did he get into this time?"

"Scrape is exactly how I'd describe it. He was fine when I loaded him in Phoenix but not so fine when I unloaded him at the folks' house. He has a pretty bad cut on his left side."

"Let's have a look."

She opened the trailer door. Sinbad nearly plowed over her in his haste to escape and only calmed when she had a firm hold on his lead rope. "That wasn't so bad, was it, old boy?"

Chase chuckled. "All these years and you still haven't trained that horse to trailer?"

"We were too busy working on other things."

As he well knew. He and his ex-wife, SherryAnne, had competed in horsemanship events alongside Jolyn up through their high-school graduation. SherryAnne went all the way to become Gila County Junior Rodeo Queen. Jolyn, the better rider in Chase's opinion, lost out at the last minute and had to settle for being one of SherryAnne's attendants.

"I really appreciate you seeing us. Dad told me Mom's been giving you a hard time again."

"She is, I won't lie. No court order yet, but she's threatened to see an attorney." Chase examined Sinbad's injury as he talked.

"For the record, Chase, I completely disagree with her." Jolyn laid a reassuring hand on his arm. "I always have."

"I know." He turned to give her a smile. "And it means a lot to me. Your mother is a force to be reckoned with when she chooses. Standing up to her isn't easy." Chase understood that more than most. He'd been the brick wall Dottie Sutherland had bashed into for the last nine years.

"Has she said anything around town?" Jolyn asked. She kept Sinbad quiet while Chase filled a bucket with water from the hose. "Mandy doesn't…hasn't heard…"

"Nothing as far as I know." Chase went to his truck and the custom-built compartments in the bed, where he stored veterinary supplies. He removed a pair of clippers, a bottle of disinfectant wash and sterilized cotton. "I will give your mother credit. She doesn't appear to be running off at the mouth, for which I'm grateful."

Chase set to work shaving the area around the wound, then he swabbed it clean. Sinbad behaved himself, paying little attention to Chase. Jolyn helped by distracting the horse with nose petting.

"You have every right to be angry at Mom. Maybe you should consider seeing an attorney yourself."

"I will if push comes to shove. So far, your mother is just

blowing smoke." Chase silently wondered how long that would last.

Almost since the day she learned the chance existed that her son, Steven, might be Mandy's biological parent—Chase refused to use the term *father*—she'd been pressuring Chase off and on to have DNA testing done. Thank God none of her family supported her, including Steven, who'd moved to Pineville years ago and purportedly wanted nothing to do with Mandy. But that didn't stop Dottie. Lately, she'd escalated her pressuring to a new level.

Chase had fought her and would continue to fight her night and day. Mandy was *his* daughter, had been from the moment the nurse placed the squirming and squalling newborn in his arms. The only way Steven or any of the Sutherlands were going to get their hands on her was over his cold, lifeless body.

"Sutures or no sutures?" he asked Jolyn.

"What do you recommend?"

"Your choice. The wound will heal without them. Might take longer, especially if it breaks open, which is likely, being near the shoulder. Depends a lot on him and how quiet you can keep him for the next several days."

"Not very. You know Sinbad."

"Yeah, I do. He won't stand well when I anesthetize the area. Which, if we decide to suture the wound, means I'd have to sedate him."

"No, you won't. He'll stand."

"You sure?" Chase squinted one eye at Jolyn.

She nodded. "He's gotten a lot better."

"Really?" Chase remained unconvinced.

"Injuries were a pretty regular occurrence in the show. Horses didn't enter the ring unless they were cleared by a vet, even when they weren't injured. The management had a strict policy."

"Okay, then. Sutures it is. Do you want to tie up one of his legs just to be on the safe side?"

"Only if you're afraid he'll kick you."

"Are you?" Chase remembered Sinbad's exit from the trailer.

"No."

Jolyn answered with such assurance, Chase laid his concerns about Sinbad's notorious high spirits to rest. Maybe age and experience had mellowed the horse.

Even so, Chase didn't once let his guard down while he cleansed and then anesthetized the affected area by injecting serum under the skin with a small needle. Because the cut was clean and recent, he trimmed away only a minimum of dead tissue.

Sinbad stood like a champ during the entire procedure. Chase finished up by applying a dressing.

"If he rubs this off, don't worry. The antibiotics are more important than the dressing."

He handed Jolyn a bottle containing a supply of metronidazole and instructed her on how many tablets to administer and how often. She was no stranger to horse care and nodded knowingly as he talked.

"If the sutures should pull loose for any reason," he continued, "or if the wound appears infected, call me."

"When do the stitches need to come out?"

"Ten, twelve days."

"I'll bring him by."

Thereby saving Chase a trip to the Sutherlands' place and a possible confrontation with Dottie. "Thanks."

"How much do I owe you?"

"I'll mail you a bill."

"You'd better." She wagged a finger at him in warning.

"I will."

"Good." Jolyn tugged on Sinbad's lead rope. "This way, buddy. Time to go back in that nasty trailer." She smiled apologetically at Chase. "He's a little sick of traveling. So am I."

"Why don't you leave him here overnight?" Chase made

the offer without thinking. Common sense told him he should cool his acquaintance with Jolyn until her mother backed off. "You can come collect him in the morning."

"Thanks." Jolyn's face brightened, making Chase glad he'd spoken first and thought later.

They walked down the barn aisle, Jolyn leading Sinbad. Head held high, ears pricked forward, the horse took in his not-unfamiliar surroundings. Once, years ago, he'd spent a lot of time in Chase's barn.

So had Jolyn. Without being told where to go, she took the horse to the line of stalls. Nickering from the barn's various occupants greeted them every step of the way. Chase opened the door to an empty stall on the end. Next, he went around the side of the barn to where the hay was stacked and grabbed two generous flakes.

When he returned, he dropped the hay into the empty feeder and turned on the spigot to the water trough. Sinbad buried his nose in the hay, snorting lustily.

Chase lifted his foot and rested it on the bottom rung of the stall's railing. So did Jolyn. They watched Sinbad eat and drink, enjoying a moment of companionable silence.

"How long you staying?" Chase asked, breaking the lull.

"Depends."

"On what?"

"On how business goes."

"What business is that?"

She smiled, and he heard pride in her voice when she said, "Sutherland Construction Company."

"No fooling!"

"No fooling. I flew into Phoenix a couple months ago and tested for my contractor's license. As of May thirty-first, I'm official."

"Congratulations. I heard you were taking some classes in Dallas. I didn't know what kind."

"Trade school. I enrolled after the accident. Had to do something with myself during all those months of physical therapy." She gave a little shrug as if it were nothing.

Chase doubted three separate knee surgeries and endless months of physical therapy were nothing. "I never pegged you for going into construction. How'd you wind up in that field?"

"We did most of our own construction in the show. Built and repaired sets and props. I found out I liked hammering nails and sawing two-by-fours—was actually good at it. Eventually, I was promoted to crew boss. Later, while I was in school, I worked part-time as a junior project manager for a commercial contractor."

"Wow." Chase eyed Jolyn with new appreciation. Though he shouldn't be surprised by her success. She'd always been the determined sort, as her rebound from a devastating injury proved. "I'm impressed."

"Well, running my own business is a far cry from running a ragtag construction crew or sitting behind a desk, punching numbers. I figure starting out in Blue Ridge where there aren't so many good ol' boys will be easier than starting out in Dallas."

"What? The boys don't take kindly to a woman muscling in on their territory?"

"I need to prove myself, and I'm okay with that. But I'd rather start out climbing a hill and not a mountain if I can help it. Once I get two or three decent jobs under my belt, generate some positive cash flow, I'll relocate to a larger market, like Pineville."

"Plenty of work around here."

"Enough to get started. But I'd like to grow my business into something more than just the local handyman."

"Hmm." This time, Chase *did* think before he spoke. And despite the warning bells clanging inside his head, he voiced the idea that had just occurred to him out loud. "I happen to have a set of plans on my kitchen table for a small-animal clinic and office. Interested in looking at them?"

"Are you serious?" Her eyes glinted with excitement.

He'd forgotten how green they looked in sunlight. And about the small dimples on each side of her mouth. "Is that a yes?"

"You're building a clinic? Where?"

"Here." He hitched a thumb at the house. "I'm expanding my practice to include small animals. And I'm hiring an assistant to help with the large animal side."

"Business must be booming."

"It helps when you have no competition."

"I'm hoping for a similar misfortune myself."

"Be ready to work yourself to death. I put in sixty to eighty hours a week. No vacations, no holidays, and forget sick days. I'm up at the crack of dawn or earlier and don't get home till seven if I'm lucky. Usually later."

"You need more than an assistant. You need an army of helpers. And you're taking on more work by expanding your practice."

"My goal is, if not to work less, at least to be around more. Sometimes I think Mandy forgets she even has a dad. If everything goes well, I'll turn over most of the large-animal practice to the assistant. Make ranch calls only in the mornings. Afternoons, I'll run the clinic here and be home when Mandy gets out of school. That way she won't have to spend so much time with babysitters."

"I bet Mandy can't wait."

"The divorce was hard on her. She misses her mother."

"But SherryAnne visits, right?"

"Once last year and that was for two days."

"I'm sorry." Jolyn's expression matched her sympathetic tone.

"Me, too. For Mandy. Personally, I could care less if

SherryAnne ever set foot in Blue Ridge again." He inadvertently tightened his grip on the railing.

Perhaps because she sensed his changing mood, Jolyn steered their conversation back to building the new clinic.

"I'd be grateful if you let me bid the job." She turned and looked him square in the face. "Even though I'm a friend, I'd expect no special consideration. Business is business."

"I have two bids already from contractors in Pineville."

"Good. That'll give you something to compare my price to and keep me honest."

"Just so you know, both prices are a little higher than what I was hoping to spend. I have a tight budget." He'd refinanced the house in order to fund the new clinic and cover the costs of hiring an assistant.

"Now, about my mother…" Jolyn grimaced.

"I won't lie, she's a thorn in my side." Chase leaned an elbow on the top railing and shifted his weight to the other foot. "She's good with Mandy, don't get me wrong. And Mandy loves dance class. Which is the only reason I let her take lessons when I'd rather keep her and your mother miles apart."

"Maybe I shouldn't bid the job."

"As you said, business is business. And this could be a mutually beneficial arrangement."

"As long as we keep my mom out of it." Jolyn gave a discouraged shake of her head. "I wouldn't put it past her to use the situation to her advantage."

Chase smiled down at Jolyn, his earlier worries melting away. Troublesome mother or not, he was glad Jolyn was back home. The affair SherryAnne had with Steven was hardly Jolyn's fault. She'd been an innocent bystander. And like he and Mandy, she was taking the brunt of the fallout.

There might once have been something between him and Jolyn back in high school, something more than friendship. It hadn't gone far, not beyond a single kiss during one of his and SherryAnne's fights. By the next day, SherryAnne had gotten her hooks back into him. She'd probably sensed the underlying attraction between him and Jolyn and refused to let it go anywhere.

He'd handled it badly with Jolyn afterward, hurting her by not fessing up right away that he and SherryAnne reconciled. Fortunately, Jolyn was understanding—more so than he deserved. And now that SherryAnne was completely out of the picture, it might be interesting to see if any of that underlying attraction remained.

"One step at a time," he told Jolyn. "First, bid the job. Then, we'll go from there." Impulsively, he took her by the arm. "Come on. I'll show you the plans. And you can say hello to Mandy. She's inside playing with a friend."

No question about it, he thought as they walked to the house. He was courting trouble by inviting Jolyn into his life.

Casting a lingering glance in her direction, he found himself warming to the idea of keeping Jolyn close. His reasons had nothing to do with her mother or building his new clinic, and everything to do with the justice she did to a pair of snug-fitting Wranglers.

Chapter Two

Jolyn stood in the middle of the stark room and evaluated her surroundings with a critical eye.

Bright midday sunlight poured in through a lone, dingy window, emphasizing the room's dismal condition. Dust particles floated in the air, thick enough to choke a snake. The faded vinyl flooring buckled in those spots where it wasn't altogether missing. Jolyn counted seven holes in the walls, the smallest one the size of her fist. Paint was a distant memory.

She didn't have to be a contractor to see that the room was a mess—and perfect for her fledgling business. Built onto the side of Cutter's Market, one of Blue Ridge's two small groceries, the room had a separate entrance and convenient parking for customers.

"Well, you want it or not?" Mrs. Cutter asked. She chewed on a plastic straw, a replacement for the cigarettes she'd given up two decades earlier.

Jolyn did want the room, but she tried not to appear overly eager—which is why she'd waited a full week after returning home to approach Mrs. Cutter about the For Rent sign in the window.

"It needs a lot of work." She ran a finger over the yellowed and cracked light-switch plate.

"Hell, yes. If it didn't, I'd have rented it out ages ago."

Jolyn pretended to consider the offer on the table. In exchange for use of the room rent free, she would be required to fix it up at no cost to Mrs. Cutter *and* make any necessary repairs to her store, also at no cost, for as long as Jolyn used the room.

"Mind if I put a lock on the door?"

"Don't bother me none as long as you give me a spare key."

"And I want a separate phone line."

"You pay for it, you got it." Mrs. Cutter leaned a shoulder on the doorjamb. Rail thin, scratchy as sandpaper, and with only a sprinkling of gray in her hair, she didn't look her age—which Jolyn guessed to be sixty-five, if not older.

"Then I suppose you have yourself a new renter."

She couldn't suppress the happiness bubbling up inside her. Sutherland Construction Company would have an honest to goodness office. When she was through fixing the place up, she'd frame her license and hang it right there next to the door where everyone could see it when they walked in.

"Do you have a lease agreement for me to sign?" she asked.

"Lease agreement?" Mrs. Cutter laughed sharply. "Good Lord, child. I've known you your whole life. Your parents for over thirty years. We only need a lease if you're thinking of breaking it."

"I'm not." Jolyn laughed along with Mrs. Cutter and extended her hand. "Can we at least shake on it?"

They no sooner clasped hands when they were joined by Jolyn's mother.

"Am I interrupting anything?" Dottie Sutherland peeked through the open door.

She was, Jolyn knew, on her way to the community center across the street where her dance class would be giving a recital that afternoon.

"Come on in," Mrs. Cutter said. "I was just leaving. Got a couple of deliveries scheduled for later today, and there ain't a lick of extra space in the back for the boxes."

"I'll be a while yet if you don't mind." Jolyn followed her new landlord outside. "I'd like to take some measurements and draw a few sketches."

"No hurry. The place is yours now." Mrs. Cutter disappeared around the corner of the building.

"Well, what do you think?" Jolyn asked her mother when she returned. Still feeling elated, she twirled in a half circle, imagining the room transformed into a functional and attractive office.

"I think you're crazy." Her mother's look of alarm said it all. "This place is a disaster area."

"The repairs are mostly cosmetic. You'd be amazed at what decent flooring and a fresh coat of paint can do."

"I don't know why you feel you need an office. What's wrong with working out of the house? You've been doing it all week."

Jolyn refused to let her mother's lack of enthusiasm ruin her mood. "I'm in the way at home. Every time you start cooking, I have to roll up my plans and clear off the kitchen table." She wanted her own desk and a visitor chair and a shelf for her reference books. "If I hope to build my business, I have to project a professional image."

"A room behind Cutter's Market isn't exactly professional."

"It's a start. And when people see my work, which they will when they come into the store, I'll draw new customers."

Maybe, she mused, she should print up some flyers and display them by the cash register. Thus far, the only two jobs she'd landed were enlarging a walk-in closet and building a new outdoor air-conditioning stand.

There was still Chase's clinic. She had the bid typed and in a folder on the front seat of her truck. He was taking a rare afternoon off work to watch Mandy perform. They'd scheduled their meeting for immediately following the recital.

Jolyn felt good about the bid, having gone over it and over

it several times. She had cut corners where she could, without cutting quality. Called every supplier in the state for the best prices. She was also planning on hiring local labor whenever possible, reducing her costs—and price—further.

If she got the job, that was.

"You've only just come home," her mother said with a catch in her voice, "and you're leaving again."

"Is that what's bothering you?"

Jolyn had to agree with her father. Her normally bubbly mother was more emotional of late. Small things, like sentimental commercials on TV and sad songs on the radio, brought tears to her eyes. And she wasn't sleeping well. Not a night passed Jolyn didn't wake to hear her mother prowling the house. She'd broached the subject twice, but as her father predicted, she'd had no luck learning what lay at the root of her mother's odd behavior.

"I'm not moving out of the house." Jolyn squeezed her mother's shoulders. "Not for a while anyway."

In truth, she couldn't afford her own place. All her money went into Sutherland Construction Company except for the modest room and board she paid her parents.

"Good," Dottie said. "Because I love having you around again."

"And I love being around." Jolyn was surprised how easily she'd slipped back into small-town life and her corner bedroom on the second floor. After touring for so many years with the show, she wondered if the urge to wander would strike her again. With a business to consider, leaving wouldn't be easy.

Unless Sutherland Construction failed.

"I suppose with some hard work, this room could make a nice office." Dottie walked to the window, her feet crunching on the debris-covered floor. "You could put your desk here where the light is good."

"Yeah." Jolyn pointed to the opposite wall. "And another desk by the door."

"Two desks?"

"If all goes well, I'll need some office help." She studied the ceiling and the many brown spots that indicated roof leaks. The repairs to Cutter's Market might be more extensive than she'd originally anticipated. "Part-time, anyway," she said distractedly.

"I'll do it."

"What?" Jolyn lowered her gaze to meet her mother's earnest one.

"I'll work for you part-time. You don't even have to pay me."

"Ah…Mom…"

"I'm good on the computer, you know that." She ticked off items on her fingers. "I've taken care of the dance school books for over twenty-five years, was treasurer of the PTA until you finished elementary school. I'm organized. People like me. And—"

"Okay." Jolyn held up a hand. "You don't have to sell yourself to me."

"I'm sorry." Her mother took a breath and smiled weakly. "I really would like to be a part of your business. If you want me."

Jolyn knew she should think carefully before answering. Her mother could, and possibly did, have an ulterior motive, especially if Jolyn won the bid for Chase's clinic. She'd avoided the subject of Mandy's parentage since her father broke the news to her, but it was still there, an elephant in the room they couldn't ignore forever.

Or, she mused, perhaps her mother's motive was no more devious than wanting to be a part of her much-absent daughter's life. Jolyn could only hope.

"I suppose we could see how it goes," she acknowledged without actually committing.

"I happen to know there's a file cabinet for sale in the thrift store. And Office Central in Pineville is having a big sale this weekend. You could pick up a desk for half price."

"Really? I'll have to check it out when I run up there for supplies."

Dottie glanced at her watch. "I'd better head on over to the community center. Some of the mothers are meeting me there early to help with costumes."

"Break a leg."

"Any chance you can swing by?"

"I wouldn't miss it."

"Oh, good." Her mother beamed, making Jolyn glad she'd decided to go.

When she was younger, she and her brother were forced to sit through every recital even after Jolyn stopped taking lessons. Today, she was looking forward to watching the twenty or so young students prance across the stage in pink tutus and purple leotards. It would be a handy distraction and keep her from fixating on her upcoming meeting with Chase.

Dottie fished her car keys from her purse. "Look, about my issue with Chase and Mandy…"

Of all the times for her mother to quit ignoring the elephant, why did she have to do it now? Jolyn pressed a hand to her churning stomach. "You know I don't agree with you."

"Yes, well, neither does your father."

"Then why not leave Chase and Mandy alone? They deserve to be happy after the hell SherryAnne put them through."

"Because that little girl could be my granddaughter," her mother said with such wrenching emotion, Jolyn was taken aback. "Your niece."

"I don't mean to sound callous, Mom, but it's not like you're going to be grandchildless your whole life."

"Neither you nor Steven have any immediate plans of getting married. And with you pouring all your time and energy into the construction company," she said, gesturing distract-edly, "I don't see you settling down and raising a family."

At least her mother didn't list the accident and resulting limp as a reason for Jolyn's current single status. "I'm twenty-nine years old," she said. "There's no hurry."

"Steven was starting kindergarten when I was your age and you were in preschool."

"Things are different now. Couples wait until they're more established before having kids."

"Leaving grandparents too old to enjoy their grandchildren!"

"You're not that old, Mom." Jolyn barely refrained from chuckling at her mother's exaggeration. "Besides, Steven might come through for you soon. He and Bethany have been living together for a while now."

Her mother rolled her eyes. "I don't see that relationship going anywhere."

"What's wrong with Bethany?" Jolyn had recently met her brother's girlfriend and thought she was nice.

"She's so much younger than your brother and still in college. I doubt she'll be interested in getting married for a while yet."

Jolyn couldn't argue that point so she tried a different approach. "Steven doesn't believe Mandy is his daughter and, let's be honest, doesn't want her. He's made that crystal clear from the beginning."

"He's avoiding the situation. He always has."

"He's being realistic and reasonable." Which was more than Jolyn could say about her mother. "Chase is Mandy's father. He loves her. If you keep pressuring him, you could wind up destroying three lives and hurting God knows how many more people, including yourself."

"I don't want to take Mandy away from Chase. I simply want to acknowledge her as my granddaughter and have visitation rights. She's a lovely little girl." Genuine fondness shone in her mother's eyes. "Very sweet and so bright. She reminds me of you when you were her age."

"Mom." Jolyn didn't understand what had prompted her mother's renewed obsession with Mandy. Maybe she was jealous of her friends and the grandchildren they were bouncing on their knees. "Chase says you've seen an attorney."

"Last month. He wasn't very helpful."

"What did he say?"

"As long as Chase refuses to have the DNA testing done and SherryAnne says he's the father, there's nothing I can do."

What a relief. "Sounds to me like you should take his advice and drop the matter." Jolyn headed toward the door, intending to retrieve her notepad from the truck so she could start on the measurements and sketches.

Her mother trailed after her. "I'm not sure I can."

Jolyn stopped and spun around. Behind her, cars pulled in and out of the market's parking lot, forcing her to raise her voice. "What's gotten into you lately?"

"Why do you keep asking me the same question over and over?"

"Because I can't help thinking that something's wrong." Jolyn softened her voice. "Please, Mom. I want to help."

Their eyes met, and for a fraction of a second Jolyn thought her mother might finally reveal what was upsetting her. Instead, she dismissed Jolyn with a flippant, "I'm fine. Perfect, in fact."

Jolyn knew better but until her mother chose to confide in her, there wasn't much she could do.

Heaving a sigh, she said, "I really wish you'd quit making trouble for Chase. He doesn't deserve it."

"You're siding with him because you've always liked him."

"I'm siding with Mandy. And of course I like Chase. We're friends."

"There was a time back in high school you wanted to be more than his friend."

"That's ridiculous. There was never anything between me and Chase."

Even as she protested her mother's assertion, Jolyn remembered the kiss she and Chase had shared that night on her parents' front porch. It had meant nothing to him, but for a few days Jolyn had foolishly hoped he'd leave SherryAnne for her.

"All I'm asking is that you not let your feelings for Chase cloud your judgment when it comes to the possibility of Mandy being my granddaughter."

Between her upcoming meeting with Chase and the conversation with her mother, Jolyn's nerves were stretched to their limit. "Let me ask you this, Mom," she snapped. "Are you willing to confront that little girl and tell her the man who raised her, the man she adores and calls Daddy, isn't her father?"

"That's not a fair question."

"Yes, it is. And until you're ready to live with the guilt of breaking two innocent people's hearts, you have no right to demand Chase have the DNA testing done."

Her mother gave her a look that was both woeful and unyielding. "If it comes to that, and I truly hope it doesn't, I'll be ready."

JOLYN PUSHED OPEN the door to the community center and entered a packed house. At least a hundred family members and friends had shown up to watch the semiannual dance recital.

Since there were no vacant seats in the front rows, she sat near the back. Catching sight of several familiar faces, she smiled and nodded in response to waves of greeting. She noted more than one whispered conversation taking place behind the shield of a raised hand. Was it her recent return that had tongues wagging? Her accident? Her brother's affair with the local vet's ex-wife? Or was her imagination working overtime?

Probably a little of each.

Thankfully, the lights dimmed and a parade of costumed girls entered the small stage from behind a curtain. Video cameras by the dozen were turned on and aimed at the stage.

The recital lasted almost an hour, ending with a thunderous round of applause. As people milled about, Jolyn remained seated, watching her mother from a distance.

Dottie was in her element. Surrounded by parents and students, she radiated pride while graciously accepting congratulations. Without missing a beat, she complimented each child, praising their talent and hard work. Heads were patted, pigtails tugged and chins pinched.

Jolyn found herself smiling. People did like her mother, and she probably would make a decent, if not darn good, secretary.

"They're talking Tony nominations backstage," a low and unmistakably male voice said from behind her. A pair of strong, tanned hands gripped the back of her chair on either side of her shoulders.

Chase.

A tiny shiver of awareness swept through Jolyn.

"Mandy did a fantastic job for someone who's only taken lessons a short time." She swiveled in her seat to find him looking down at her, his face mere inches away, his dark brown eyes studying her intently.

Chase didn't appear to be affected by their proximity. And neither was she. Not in the least. She was pulling at the collar of her blouse only because the material itched.

"Mandy wants to hang out with her friends for a few minutes," he said. "I thought maybe we could sit at one of the picnic tables outside and go over your bid. Unless you'd rather meet someplace less casual."

"The picnic tables are fine."

Jolyn and Chase walked down their individual rows and met up in the center aisle.

"Give me a minute to let Mandy know where we'll be."

"Sure thing."

Chase touched Jolyn's arm. No more than a brush of his fingers, really. So why did it feel like so much more? She watched him slowly weave his way toward the stage.

With his six-foot-two frame, black hair and shoulders rivaling those of a professional athlete, he was easy to track even in a large crowd. If that weren't enough, his long-sleeved blue denim work shirt stood out in a sea of T-shirts and tank tops. He must have come straight from a call to the recital.

"Hello, Jolyn."

She turned and came face-to-face with Susan and Joseph Raintree, Chase's aunt and uncle. "Hi. How are you?" Collecting her scattered wits, she shook hands with both of them.

"Welcome home," Susan said kindly. She could have snubbed Jolyn as easily. Perhaps the Raintrees weren't aware of her mother's latest campaign. Chase had mentioned Dottie being closemouthed. "How long are you staying?"

"I'm not sure." Everyone Jolyn ran into asked her the same question. She gave her stock answer. "Depends on how business goes." If she didn't get some decent jobs soon, she might be gone before the end of summer. "How's your family?" she inquired instead.

Susan glowed. "Great. Gage and Aubrey got married this spring. They're both working and couldn't be here."

"Tell them congratulations for me, please."

Jolyn remembered Chase's cousin Gage well, though he'd been less interested in rodeoing than Chase and more into sports during their high-school days. She knew Aubrey only slightly but liked her.

"Hannah's going to Pineville College, studying ranch management." Susan crossed her fingers. "She should graduate at the end of fall semester if she can pass all her classes."

"You ready to leave?" Joseph grumbled.

He'd obviously reached his tolerance of squealing little girls and effusive, chatty parents.

Susan rolled her eyes. "It was nice seeing you again." She linked her arm through Joseph's and smiled up at him softly.

"Same here."

Jolyn was immediately joined by a former classmate. The woman had a five-year-old daughter in the recital and was quick to mention she also had a son. Jolyn wondered how many of her old friends were now married with families. Could this be why her mother had become obsessed with having a grandchild?

"Sorry to take so long." Chase returned just as her old friend was leaving. He stood close to Jolyn, not that he had to. The crowd was thinning with each passing second. "Shall we?" He motioned toward the door.

Jolyn nodded, her throat suddenly dry. Here, at last, was the moment of truth. Her first official bid presentation to a prospective client. How well it went could affect many things, including the duration of her stay in Blue Ridge and if she could make a go of Sutherland Construction Company.

She might feel more confident about the outcome if her mother weren't trying to wreck Chase's life.

Chapter Three

Chase opened the back door to his aunt and uncle's house and hollered, "Anybody home?"

"Come in," his cousin Hannah called.

Mandy squeezed in ahead of him, making a sweeping entrance into the kitchen. She was still wearing her recital costume and riding high from all the excitement.

"Did you see the show, Aunt Hannah?" she asked, executing an awkward but charming pirouette.

"No, sweetie, I didn't." Hannah applauded when Mandy was done, then scooped her up for a hug. "I just got home from school. But your Aunt Susan videotaped it. We're all going to watch it after supper."

"You have to go to school?"

"'Fraid so."

"But it's summer."

"College is different. I'm trying to graduate early so I have to go during the summer. Nights and weekends, too."

Mandy made a face. "That sucks."

"Watch your language," Chase warned.

His cousin gave him a bemused glance as she released a squirming Mandy. "She's right, it does."

"Been there, done that. It's hard, but you'll get through it."

Chase had pushed himself to finish veterinary school in

record time. In his case, because he had a wife and baby daughter at home. A wife he barely talked to in those days.

Eventually, he and SherryAnne managed to tolerate each other. Even to get along at times. When SherryAnne announced she was divorcing him and leaving Blue Ridge to pursue a career as a professional barrel racer, Chase was disappointed, but not surprised. They'd agreed when Mandy was born to stick it out so that their daughter would have the benefit of being raised by two parents. That commitment had lasted seven years.

They'd never fought for custody. SherryAnne wanted her freedom and Chase wanted his daughter. *His* daughter. No one else's.

Chase had learned about SherryAnne's infidelity by accident early in her pregnancy. He'd stayed with her until Mandy was born, planning to have DNA testing done soon after. It proved unnecessary. Chase didn't need a test to tell him what he knew in his heart to be true.

"Hey there, you two." Chase's Aunt Susan came into the kitchen and ooh'd and aah'd appropriately when Mandy spontaneously performed part of her dance routine. "Aubrey just got off work," she said after Mandy curtsied. "She and Gage are picking up pizza from Sage's Bar and Grill on their way back from town."

"Pizza, pizza," Mandy singsonged and went in search of Chase's Uncle Joseph to give yet another miniperformance to an admiring fan.

"She's so cute." Susan smiled dotingly. She and Joseph had become like substitute grandparents to Mandy after Chase's parents had moved to Mesa. They still visited but only occasionally, usually around the holidays. Chase rarely had time off to visit them, something he hoped to change. As a result, Mandy spent a lot of time at the ranch. Chase, too, when he could get away. "You probably aren't crazy about me saying this," Susan went on, "but she's the spitting image of SherryAnne."

"She is." Chase couldn't deny the obvious. Mandy, with her red hair and freckles, had always favored her mother, for which he was glad.

His greatest concern was that Mandy might hear disturbing gossip about her mother or become the object of taunts and teasing. Protecting her 24/7 was beyond his abilities. Neither could he bring himself to tell her about her mother's affair before someone else did. She was too young and too vulnerable.

A year between visits from SherryAnne had been hard on Mandy. Seeing her dancing around the kitchen in her recital costume, grinning from ear to ear, gave Chase hope that she would eventually rebound from her mother's abandonment.

He hated to admit it, but he was thankful to Dottie Sutherland. She and her dance classes had restored some of the missing light in his daughter's eyes. Dottie had also, as promised, not said one word to Mandy about her mother's affair with Steven.

"I saw Jolyn at the dance recital." Aunt Susan removed a stack of paper plates from the cupboard. "She looks good."

Pulling one of the chairs away from the table, Chase dropped down into it. "She does."

"Except for the limp, you'd never know what she's been through the last year. I heard she had to learn to walk all over again."

"I heard she almost lost her leg," Hannah said.

"Imagine taking up a profession where you spend half your time outdoors and on your feet after something like that." Susan shook her head in amazement. "She's one strong gal."

Chase thought of Jolyn while his aunt and cousin set the table. He'd forgotten about her limp. He'd been too busy noticing other things about her, like the long, smooth line of her legs and the hands that looked too soft and delicate to bang a hammer or saw wood.

Never one to hem and haw, Hannah asked, "Did she give you the bid for your clinic?"

"Yeah. We went over it after the recital."

"And…"

Both his cousin and aunt stopped what they were doing to stare at him expectantly.

"And her price is almost fifteen percent under the next lowest bid."

Hannah whistled. "That's a lot of money."

"It's not just the money. She included several items in her bid the other two contractors missed."

Jolyn had impressed Chase with her attention to detail. Unlike the other two contractors he'd dealt with, she'd patiently explained all the components of the bid in everyday terms he could understand.

"Money's not everything," Aunt Susan cautioned. "There's experience and reputation to consider. She doesn't have much of either, I'm guessing."

"You're right. She did provide me with several references, though, including the Wild and Wooly West manager and her former boss at the commercial contractor in Dallas. I called both of them earlier. They gave her glowing recommendations."

"That's to be expected." Aunt Susan removed a pitcher of iced tea from the refrigerator. "A person doesn't give out names of people who won't talk them up."

"True. But I did ask a lot of questions, described exactly what I'm building. Both men expressed their confidence in her abilities."

Aunt Susan sat in the chair across from Chase. "I have no right interfering in your life, so feel free to tell me to butt out." She lowered her voice and directed her gaze to the family room. Mandy continued to entertain her great uncle, who was trying his best to watch her and the six o'clock news at the same time. "I know Jolyn is your friend, but she's also

Dottie's daughter. Working closely with her could lead to trouble. Big trouble."

"Believe me, I know." Chase rubbed the back of his neck, massaging the kinks loose. "But Jolyn supports me where Mandy is concerned. She always has."

"Are you absolutely sure? Family ties are strong."

"Pretty sure," Chase answered honestly.

"Dottie could try and use Jolyn to get to you without Jolyn realizing it."

"Jolyn's aware of her mother's goals and I think she's savvy enough to not let herself be manipulated."

"In my opinion," Hannah said, "you're safe using Jolyn. She needs this job if she wants her business to succeed, and she won't do anything to screw it up. Neither will Dottie."

Hannah looked at her mother as if challenging her to disagree. Susan gave a noncommittal shrug.

"I like that she's here in town." Chase leaned back and stretched out his cramped legs. He wasn't used to sitting as much as he had this afternoon. "The other two contractors admitted that while workers may be on the job every day, they would only make the trip from Pineville two or three times a week. If something were to go wrong, Jolyn would be five minutes away."

"It's cool you're giving a woman a shot at this. And the money you'd save…" Hannah rubbed her thumb and first two fingers together. "You can do a lot with all that extra green stuff."

Chase quickly added some numbers in his head. "I can pay for the holding kennels, waiting room furniture and a three-year lease on an X-ray machine."

Susan rose from the table. "Sounds like you've decided." The tiny hint of disapproval in her tone was unmistakable.

"Not yet," Chase said. "I'm going to sleep on it tonight. See how I feel tomorrow."

"I'm glad you're taking your time deciding."

From outside came the sounds of tires on gravel and the Raintrees' pet dog, Biscuit, barking. Gage and Aubrey had arrived with the pizza.

Hannah grinned knowingly at Chase and said too softly for her mother to hear, "When are you going to tell Jolyn she has the job?"

"In the morning." He grinned back at her. "She's bringing Sinbad by early to have his sutures removed."

She jumped up to give her mother a hand with dinner and patted Chase's shoulder as she walked by. "You've made the right decision, cuz."

Chase thought so, too. There were any number of reasons why he shouldn't award the job to Sutherland Construction Company and an equal number of reasons why he should. Granted, he might be taking a chance, but his gut told him to hire Jolyn.

And besides, he rather liked the idea of working with her. It felt right, and nothing had felt right for Chase in a long, long time.

JOLYN PULLED BACK on Sinbad's reins, squeezed gently with her legs and commanded him to walk in a firm voice. He obeyed and slowed from a fast trot, but not willingly. She didn't blame him. Between the trip from Dallas and his latest injury, two weeks had passed since she'd last ridden him.

Sinbad disliked confinement. He was an athletic animal, taking pleasure in racing from one end of the arena to the other or leaping over obstacles most horses would refuse. Advancing age had affected his ability somewhat, but not his desire. If Jolyn were to give him his head, he'd gallop the entire half mile to Chase's house.

Instead, they walked. Because of her, not him.

Jolyn hadn't raced or jumped or done anything more demanding than a controlled lope around the bullpen since the accident. She hadn't ridden Sinbad at all until four months ago and then she'd done it against doctor's orders. But if she hadn't climbed onto Sinbad's back soon, she might never have gotten on a horse again.

Sometimes, Jolyn dreamed about the fall. In her dreams, she and Sinbad were flying over the wagon, just as they'd done in every performance for nine straight years. The crowd held their breath in collective anticipation.

Suddenly, the silence was shattered by the sharp *thwack* of Sinbad's hoof hitting the side of the wagon. She felt his broad body shift beneath her as he was thrown off balance, saw the ground rush up to meet her, heard the sickening crunch when she hit and her own low "Oomph."

Agonizing pain shot up her leg, so fierce it literally blinded her. She had no time to recover before Sinbad toppled like a giant oak tree and rolled on top of her, pinning her beneath a thousand pounds of thrashing, terrified horse.

She was told later that in clawing his way to his feet, Sinbad had injured her further. Broken ribs, a separated shoulder and torn ligaments were only a few of the injuries she'd suffered. Jolyn didn't remember. She'd lost consciousness well before then.

She'd replayed the accident often enough to know it was just that: an accident. It could have happened to anyone at any time. Unfortunately, it had happened to her and changed the course of her life forever. She was lucky. It could have ended her life.

Jolyn rode bareback today, another reason she held Sinbad to a walk and probably why she was thinking about the accident. She'd decided against putting a saddle on him, afraid the cinch might aggravate his injury.

All at once, Sinbad lifted his head and whinnied shrilly. He recognized their destination, having traveled this same route countless times, and no coaxing on Jolyn's part could keep him from breaking into a fast trot.

They reached Chase's barn just as the sun crested the distant mountains. Jolyn loved morning rides and was glad when Chase suggested she come by early to have Sinbad's wound examined and the sutures removed.

Their meeting the previous afternoon had gone well. At least, *she* thought so. Chase gave no indication of how her bid stacked up against the other two, telling her he'd let her know his decision in a few days.

The wait would be excruciating. No matter how tempting, she was resolved not to mention the bid or the clinic this morning, even if she had to spend the entire visit biting her tongue.

Chase must have heard Sinbad's hooves clip-clopping up his driveway, for he came out from around the side of the house at the same moment she was dismounting. Slowly. Jolyn's feet touched ground, and she cemented her teeth together to avoid crying out. She led Sinbad around in a small circle, as much to settle him as to walk off the pain in her knee.

"There," she said to Sinbad in a whispery voice, "that wasn't so bad."

Chase reached her a few seconds later, a steaming mug of coffee in his outstretched hand. "Morning."

"You're a lifesaver." She took the mug with fingers that were stiff from constantly yanking on Sinbad's reins.

"Hope you still take it with cream and sugar."

"I've learned to take it any way I can get it, but I still prefer cream and sugar." She raised the mug to her lips. The coffee was warm but not hot, and she drank several large swallows.

"So, how's our boy doing?"

"Good, I think." Jolyn led Sinbad over to the hitching post just inside the barn.

Chase stood beside her, examining Sinbad's wound.

Using his thumb and fingers, he pushed in on the sutures and grunted with satisfaction. "It's healing nicely. No infection or tearing, and scarring should be minimal. How much of the antibiotics are left?"

"Two days' worth."

"Finish them off to be on the safe side."

He went to his truck, opened one of the compartments and returned with a large wad of cotton, a bottle of some kind of medicine and an odd-looking pair of scissors. After swabbing the injured area, he deftly and quickly removed the stitches. Sinbad's only reaction was to snake his head around to see what all the fuss was about.

While Chase was bent over swabbing the area a second time, he said, "When could you start construction on my office?"

"What?" Jolyn wasn't sure she'd heard him correctly.

He straightened, his expression serious except for a barely noticeable crinkling at the corners of his eyes. "When could you start construction?"

Jolyn's heart kicked into overdrive. "Um…right away. As soon as the permit's ready." She cautioned herself not to jump to conclusions. Chase hadn't awarded her the job. He'd only inquired about a start date.

"The permit can be picked up anytime. I just need to give the county the name of the general contractor." The smile lighting his eyes spread to his mouth. "Which I guess is going to be Sutherland Construction."

"Really?"

"Yes, really."

She started to hug Chase, then caught herself. Contractors didn't hug their brand-new clients. "Thank you, Chase. You won't be disappointed, I promise. I've already put together a tentative schedule just in case and lined up three workers to handle—" She abruptly stopped, realizing she was rambling.

Striving to speak slowly, she asked, "Would you like me to drive into Globe today and pick up the permit?"

"Do you mind?"

"Of course not." Jolyn had pulled many permits for the contractor in Dallas. None with her own name on them, though. "I'll leave this morning." Globe, the county seat, was a good twenty minutes farther away than Pineville and in the opposite direction.

"What's next?" Chase asked.

Jolyn led Sinbad out of the barn, Chase walking beside her. They stopped beside the fence to continue their conversation. "We should sign a contract. What kind depends on your lender, if you have one, and their requirements."

"No lender."

"Then we have a few options. How about I bring the permit and paperwork by this afternoon? In the meantime, I'll contact the concrete company, see when's the earliest they can start."

"Better wait until early evening to come over. I have a full day because of taking yesterday afternoon off. I'll phone when I'm heading home."

"Sounds good." Jolyn began mentally planning her day. "Don't forget. You'll need to clear the construction area. I can help tonight."

"I think I can handle it." He reached into his back pocket for his wallet and removed a business card. "Here. My cell phone's on that in case you need to get hold of me for any reason."

Jolyn took the card and ran her thumb along the crisp edge. The magnitude of the last few minutes sank in, filling her with joy. Thanks to Chase, she had her first big job. Sutherland Construction Company was no longer a dream. She pocketed Chase's business card, resisting the urge to fling her arms wide and laugh out loud.

Sinbad nudged her elbow with his nose.

"Somebody's ready to go home," she said, hoping Chase didn't notice the giddy tremor in her voice. "Got something around here I can use as a step up?" Without a saddle and stirrups, Jolyn couldn't climb onto Sinbad unassisted.

"I'll help you." He bent and linked his fingers together.

Hesitantly, Jolyn reached out and placed her hand on Chase's shoulder. It was strong and wider than she remembered, the fabric of his work shirt warm from the morning sun. Lifting her left leg, she placed her booted foot in his cupped hands and prayed her right leg wouldn't buckle under the strain.

In the next instant, Chase boosted her onto Sinbad's back, just like he had countless times when they were younger. Only today, his large and very capable hand lingered on the back of her calf.

Sensation flowed up Jolyn's leg, more electrifying than it should be under the circumstances. Chase was her client, her veterinarian, her old friend. But his hand on her leg evoked a response in her that had little to do with business and friendship.

Sinbad pawed the ground, eager to start home.

"Take it easy with this big boy for another week or two," Chase said, still holding Jolyn's leg. "Don't gallop or jump him if you can avoid it."

"No problem." She hadn't done either of those things since the accident.

"I'll see you tonight, then." He squeezed her calf, then stepped back.

Jolyn waved. She didn't trust herself to speak.

Chapter Four

Jolyn stepped back and out of the way as the last of the wet concrete was poured to create the foundation of Chase's new clinic.

A moment later, the friendly-faced young driver who'd made the delivery handed Jolyn a receipt attached to a clipboard. "If I could just get your signature, ma'am, I'll be outta here."

She inspected the quantity and the total dollar amount before signing off. The delivery charge was twice the normal rate, but expected. Traveling the road from Pineville to Blue Ridge was both hazardous and time-consuming, forcing her to pay a premium.

"Thank you." She returned the clipboard after removing the customer copy for her records.

"My pleasure." The young man's gaze lingered on her a second or two longer than necessary before he turned and left.

He wasn't the only one to stare at her with undisguised interest. Jolyn had received similar looks from the clerk at the county office when she pulled the permit, two of the framers and the guy who operated the front-end loader when they'd excavated the ground. His daughter had once competed against Jolyn in barrel-racing events.

Evidently, men in these parts weren't accustomed to deal- ing with a woman contractor. Their interest ranged from blatantly sexual to mildly curious. And while no one had shown her any disrespect, a few of the men had been borderline condescending. If that was the worst treatment she received, she'd consider herself lucky.

Jolyn walked the perimeter of the foundation and watched the trio of finishers with their long-handled bull floats transform the rough bed of concrete into a smooth, clean expanse. In this heat, the concrete would solidify within a couple of hours. Tomorrow, they would start framing the exterior walls.

Confident everything was going well, she went to her truck. Opening one of the side-mounted toolboxes, she dug around for a tape measure and a level, which, to her annoyance, weren't in the last place she'd left them.

She heard Mandy's small voice behind her.

"Whatcha doing?"

"Hey there." Jolyn extracted the tape measure with a triumphant grin. "I'm looking for this. And a level. What are you doing?"

"Nothing. I'm bored."

Two dogs sat at Mandy's heels, purple and pink leashes attached to their collars. One was short, squat and pitifully ugly, the other a shepherd mix with half of one ear missing. As a kid, Chase was forever dragging home stray or injured animals. Jolyn suspected not much had changed in that regard.

"Can I watch you work for a while?"

"If it's okay with your dad." She thought Mandy looked more unhappy than bored.

"He's still inside talking to Mrs. Payne. She's watching me today," Mandy said. "After she's done washing the dishes and folding the laundry, she's taking me to her house. She doesn't have satellite TV, you know."

"Bummer." Jolyn resumed rummaging in the toolbox for the level.

"Yeah." Mandy sighed.

"What about games?" Jolyn asked, wondering if the lack of satellite TV was the only reason for Mandy's dejection.

"Mrs. Payne doesn't play games. She sews quilts."

Jolyn finally located the level, which was buried at the very bottom. "Let me guess. You don't like to sew quilts."

"I like to dance."

"I saw you at the recital last week. You were good." When Jolyn crossed the yard to the concrete pad, Mandy and the dogs followed her.

"Are you a dancer?"

"Me? No." Jolyn caught the attention of the closest finisher and pointed to a rough patch that needed smoothing. "I took lessons for a while, then quit." She winked at Mandy. "I didn't have your talent."

"Dad says you and him used to show horses together. Mommy, too."

"That's right," Jolyn said distractedly. With some difficulty, she knelt on the ground and lowered her head until it was even with the pad, visually inspecting it. "Your mom and I were best friends."

"You were!"

Jolyn cranked her head around. "Your dad didn't tell you?"

"No." Mandy's face reflected a mixture of surprise, delight and disappointment. "He said you were friends, but not *best* friends."

"Since we were younger than you." Jolyn tried to stand but her right leg refused to support her weight. Wincing with pain, she braced her hands on her bent left knee and waited a moment to catch her breath before trying to rise again.

"You okay?" Mandy asked.

"My leg's a little sore today."

Sore didn't begin to describe how it felt. Jolyn had been pushing herself hard for weeks now—driving great distances, walking more than usual, tackling the repairs at Cutter's Market and her new office and riding Sinbad whenever she had a spare hour.

"Need help?" Mandy took Jolyn by the elbow and tugged.

Despite the little girl's spindly arms, she impressed Jolyn by managing to hoist her to her feet.

"Those dance lessons have obviously paid off."

"What?" Mandy furrowed her small, freckled brow.

"I was making a joke." Huffing, Jolyn smoothed the girl's hair. "Evidently a bad one."

"Dad says you hurt your leg when you fell from your horse but I'm not supposed to ask you about it because you might be…" She scrunched her mouth to one side. "Sensitive."

Jolyn laughed. "You can ask me any questions you want. I don't mind."

"I'd rather you tell me about my mother."

She really should get back to work, but the desperation on Mandy's face tugged at Jolyn's heart. She didn't understand how SherryAnne could leave her child behind and visit only once during the last two years. Surely professional rodeo riders got vacations once in a while.

"You look like her."

"Everybody tells me that."

"It's true." Jolyn's mother was deluding herself if she thought she saw something of Jolyn in Mandy. "But you act more like your dad."

"He didn't eat his vegetables, either?"

"Okay," Jolyn conceded, "there may be a few differences between you."

"And he likes horses more than I do. I've got a pony and everything, but I'd rather dance."

No, Mandy was definitely not the least bit like Jolyn. "You're nice like he is. And sweet. Kind of quiet, too, until you get to know somebody."

SherryAnne had always been a loud whirlwind of a person, who existed at the center of her own world. She'd alternate between lavishing affection on her friends and snubbing them.

Her and Jolyn's relationship had been a complex one—they were friends, but also rivals. Jolyn diligently kept that rivalry restricted to the horse arena, refusing to let it involve Chase. She'd clearly made the right decision, because she and Chase had remained close through the years.

The same wasn't true for her and SherryAnne. They'd hardly spoken after SherryAnne's affair with Steven was discovered and not at all since Jolyn left Blue Ridge.

"What did you and Mommy do together?"

Jolyn concentrated on the good memories, those before high school when Chase went from being a boy in their class to SherryAnne's love interest.

"You probably won't believe this but your mom adored Barbie dolls. I think she must have had five or six and a few of Barbie's friends."

Mandy's face lit up. "I have Barbies, too."

"When we were a little older, we used to go to Cutter's Market pretty much every day. Mostly we rode our horses but sometimes we took our bikes or walked. You mom would buy the latest teen magazine and cut out pictures of all the cute boys. Then she'd tape the pictures to the wall behind her bed."

"Really?" Mandy's tone suggested she didn't understand the appeal. "I have pictures of ballerinas on my wall."

"I had pictures of horses."

Mandy giggled. "Do you have any brothers or sisters?"

The question came so far from left field it gave Jolyn a start. "Yes," she answered cautiously.

"Which," Mandy persisted, "and how many of each?"

"One. A brother."

Jolyn started walking the perimeter of the pad again,

checking for defects. Mandy and her small parade of dogs kept pace alongside her.

"Does he live here in Blue Ridge?"

"No. Pineville." Jolyn cast furtive glances at the back door, hoping Chase would appear and give her a reason not to talk about her brother. When he didn't, she improvised. "Hey, I've got an idea."

"What?"

"Is there a stick around here?" She scanned the nearby ground.

So did Mandy. "Why?"

"You'll see." They found a short stick that would work for what Jolyn had in mind. "Come on."

She led Mandy to a three-by-five rectangular area jutting out from the concrete pad. It would become the patient entrance when the building was complete.

Jolyn stooped over and, using the end of the stick, scratched the date and Mandy's name in the lower right hand corner of the rectangle.

"There. Now place your hand below your name and press really hard."

When Mandy did as instructed, Jolyn laid her own hand over Mandy's and applied more pressure. The print came out perfect, and Mandy squealed with delight.

"Can we do the dogs' prints in the other corner?"

"Sure. What are their names?"

"Buzz and Lickety."

Jolyn scratched the dogs' names beside Mandy's. Buzz and Lickety were less enthused about being immortalized in concrete than their young owner but eventually submitted. Jolyn figured if Chase objected, she'd grind out the names and prints and patch the area.

"What's going on?"

Jolyn spun around to find Chase watching them. She'd

been so absorbed with Mandy, she hadn't heard him approach.

"We were—"

"Daddy, look!" Mandy chimed in while Buzz hobbled off, shaking his foot and whining indignantly.

Chase inspected his daughter's handiwork and smiled. "Very nice."

"If you want, I can fix it later," Jolyn whispered.

"Are you kidding? It's great."

"Daddy, let's do your handprint, too."

"That's okay, kiddo. Three's enough."

Mandy jumped up and threw her arms around her father's waist. "I'm going inside to get Mrs. Payne and show her." In the next instant, she was tearing toward the back door, the dogs on her heels.

Chase turned to Jolyn. "Thanks."

"I didn't do anything."

"Yes, you did. Mandy's been having a tough go of things since her mother left. Each time I think we're making headway, something happens to set us back again. Last night SherryAnne called to say she wasn't sure she was going to be here for Mandy's birthday next month."

"Oh, Chase. I'm sorry."

"Me, too. I figured today was going to be a difficult one for all of us. Now it's not." He glanced down at the hand and dog prints. "Because of you."

Giving her no warning whatsoever, he bent and kissed her on the cheek.

Jolyn went utterly still as his lips brushed her skin. She resisted curling her arms around his neck—barely—but couldn't keep her eyes from drifting closed. When he finally straightened, Jolyn's breath fled her lungs in a slow *whoosh*.

She had no chance to recover before he said, "I'll call you later tonight," and made for the barn.

The back door banged open, cutting off Jolyn's reply. Not that she had one. The kiss, despite being chaste, stole her ability to think coherently.

Mandy came darting across the yard, Mrs. Payne in tow. They gave no indication of having seen Chase kiss Jolyn.

If only the same could be said about everybody else there.

When Jolyn finally collected her scattered wits, it was to find a half-dozen construction workers staring at her, most of them wearing silly smirks.

Great. Her face and neck burned with embarrassment. Getting cozy with her client was hardly the way to earn the respect of employees and subcontractors.

She, of all people, should know better. From now on, she'd have to act more professionally in Chase's presence.

It wouldn't be easy—not when she could still feel his lips on her skin.

DOTTIE SUTHERLAND doodled on the small notepad in front of her while waiting for her caller to return and interrupt the lame song playing in the background. Shifting the phone to her other ear, she gripped her pen tighter. More curly, swirly clouds became sharp-cornered boxes the longer she waited.

Finally, a living, breathing voice came on the line. "Sorry to keep you holding."

"That's all right." It wasn't all right but objecting would be an exercise in futility.

"Can you be here this Thursday at four-fifteen?" the caller asked in a clipped, neutral voice.

Three days. Dottie's stomach gave a small, uncomfortable lurch.

She scribbled the date above one of the doodles, wondering what excuse she could give her family for the trip to Pineville. Shopping, she supposed.

"Mrs. Sutherland?"

Dottie cleared her throat. She almost said no, but knew she couldn't postpone the appointment. Not again.

"That'll be fine. Thursday at four-fifteen. Thank you."

She disconnected the portable phone and set it on the kitchen table. Tears stung her eyes. She tried to wipe them away but all at once there were too many. Thank goodness Milt and Jolyn were both at work.

Dottie quit holding in her anger and frustration at the unfairness of it all and let herself cry. It felt good for a change. Keeping up pretenses was exhausting, as was lying to her family. But she couldn't tell them. Not yet. After Thursday, when she knew for sure, she'd say something. Maybe. God willing, she wouldn't have to.

"Sweetheart, what's wrong?"

Dottie turned her head and let out a soft gasp. Milt stood in the doorway to the kitchen.

"What are you doing here?" she asked, her heart hammering in her chest. The tears filling her eyes instantly dried.

He held out a brown paper package. "Those costume patterns you ordered came in. Thought I'd surprise you and bring them home."

Surprise was an understatement. Milt was the local postmaster and, unless he was too sick to stand, didn't take time off work.

"Who's minding the post office?"

"No one. I locked up. Figured the world wouldn't come to an end if I left an hour early." He moved toward her and set the package on the table. "Mind telling me what's the matter?"

"Nothing."

"Quit lying." Milt had apparently reached the limit of his patience, and she couldn't blame him. The poor kitchen chair took the brunt of his irritation as he jerked it out from the table and sat down. "Don't you think it's time you leveled with me?"

He stared at her, unwaveringly. Dottie resisted, until he

reached out and swept a tousled lock of hair from her face. The loving gesture did her in, snapping the last vestiges of her resistance. She'd just wanted to spare her family. It was clear, however, that her efforts were causing more harm than good.

Mustering all her courage, she said, "I found some lumps in my breasts."

When she was finished pouring out her story, Milt covered her fingers and squeezed. In an uncustomarily thick voice, he said, "I'll go with you to your appointment."

"You don't have to."

"The hell I don't," he growled.

Dottie nodded and felt a small portion of her burden lift.

Chapter Five

"Oh, wow!" Mandy stopped three feet inside the contractor superstore and looked around, wide-eyed. "This place is cool."

"A girl after my own heart," Jolyn said.

Chase didn't miss the conspiratorial smile she flashed his daughter.

Not for the first time that day he was glad he'd wrangled an invitation to accompany her to Pineville and that she'd agreed to bring Mandy along. Jolyn might be at his house every day but they'd seen little of each other in the week since construction on the clinic started.

"Who knew inside this small ballerina lurked a construction worker?" He took an awestruck Mandy by the hand and led her along. "No wandering off, you hear me? Stick close."

"Can we paint my room?"

"No, we just did that last year."

"I want a new lamp for my dresser."

"Maybe for your birthday."

"What are those things?"

"Don't touch, Mandy."

Chase heaved a tired sigh, and Jolyn laughed.

"You'll get no sympathy from me. I feel the same as Mandy every time I walk into one of these places."

She grabbed one of the large pushcarts.

"Can I ride on that?" Mandy asked, her face alight.

"No," Chase said and pulled her back before she could scramble onto the cart.

"Sorry, sweetie." Jolyn removed a list of supplies from her jeans pocket. "The store has a policy about kids riding on carts."

"Why don't I take her around the store," Chase suggested. "Keep her busy while you shop." Jolyn had mentioned needing materials for Cutter's Market and her new office, along with items for the clinic.

"Thanks. That'd be great. What say we meet in the flooring section…." She glanced at her watch. "Around two-thirty. That'll give me a good half hour."

"Two-thirty it is—"

Mandy broke free of Chase in order to climb on a riding lawn mower. His attempts to coax her down were met with resistance. When Mandy dug in her heels, she was the spitting image of SherryAnne. Only when his tone went from reasonable to stern did Mandy comply. By then, Jolyn had swung her cart around and was heading toward the opposite end of the store.

When she'd mentioned her scheduled trip to Pineville and her intention of returning with flooring, paint and cabinet samples for him to look at, Chase had surprised himself by asking to go with her. Interviewing for a new assistant had squeezed his already tight schedule and, in all honesty, he couldn't afford more time off work. But the idea of spending the afternoon with Jolyn was too tempting to pass up.

There'd been a brief moment of unease when she mentioned a personal errand, stating she didn't want to inconvenience Chase and Mandy while she was tied up. Chase suggested he take Mandy to a movie, and the uneasiness vanished, though his curiosity was admittedly piqued. Where could she be going and why?

Later it occurred to him that she might be planning to visit her brother. At the thought of Steven, Chase's mood had taken a decidedly sour turn, and if not for Mandy he'd have canceled the trip.

As it turned out, however, the three of them had enjoyed a pleasant drive up the mountain. The hour had flown by with Chase and Jolyn catching up on the intervening years and old friends. Many were still living in town but just as many had left Blue Ridge. The job market simply wasn't expanding at a rate equal to the population.

If Jolyn's construction company grew and became successful, she could provide jobs for any number of people besides herself. She'd already hired three laborers and talked of hiring more. How long she employed those people would depend on whether or not she landed more work. Chase intended to do his part in building Sutherland Construction by spreading the word.

His motives weren't entirely unselfish. For reasons he wasn't quite ready to explore, he wanted Jolyn to remain in Blue Ridge. And not just because of the employment opportunities her company created or the small boost to the local economy. Though what kind of relationship they could have—if any—depended in large part on her mother.

Dottie Sutherland had backed off considerably since Jolyn's return, but Chase knew better than to think she'd abandoned her mission. Dollars to donuts, Dottie's reprieve was temporary, and she was even now gathering her forces for her next move.

At two-thirty-five, Chase was in the flooring section, trying to interest Mandy in a book of wallpaper samples and keeping an eye out for Jolyn.

"Daddy, I'm bored."

How was that possible? Half an hour ago she'd been enthralled.

"Can I help you with something?" asked a clerk with a Check Out Our Home Decorating Packages badge on his apron bib.

"Maybe in a minute or two. I'm waiting for my..." He hesitated, not sure what to call Jolyn. She was his friend, but in this situation, she was also his contractor. "For someone."

"Holler if you need anything," the clerk said and left to consult with a clipboard-toting associate.

At the sound of a squeaky wheel, Chase turned to see Jolyn approaching, pushing an overloaded and unwieldy cart. Her limp, which had become more pronounced recently, was worse than ever. Chase hurried over to help her.

"Let me get that for you." He nudged her away from the handle. "Sit with Mandy while I find a place to park this."

She didn't object to him commandeering her cart, proving to Chase that he was right about her leg bothering her.

"Is there someplace I can leave this while we look at samples?" he asked the clerk.

"Sure. Right over here." He led Chase to a spot behind the counter. "In the market for anything special today?"

Chase nodded in Jolyn's direction. She'd taken a seat at the sample table. Mandy stood beside her, peering over her shoulder.

"Vinyl flooring. For a small-animal clinic and adjoining office."

With the cart safely stowed, they returned to the sample table.

"Any particular style in mind?"

"Something durable but reasonably priced," Chase said, quoting Jolyn.

"We have any number of good products." They reached Jolyn and Mandy, and the clerk greeted them with a hearty, "Good afternoon. How are you ladies doing?"

"Fine, thanks." In front of Jolyn was propped a large board on which were adhered dozens of four-inch tile squares in various styles and shades of color.

"I like that one." Mandy pointed to a lavender tile with streaks of yellow running through it.

"What we need is something white or possibly light grey." Jolyn tapped a tile in the top row. "This one, maybe."

Mandy made a face. "The purple one is prettier."

"Yes. And it would hide dirty paw prints and you-know-what kind of accidents better."

Mandy giggled.

"But the floor has to look bright and sterile. People want to be assured their pet will be well taken care of when they come in. White tile feels more like a hospital." She glanced up at Chase and added, "Unless you think differently."

"No." He gestured offhandedly. "Sounds to me like you've covered everything."

"How many square feet you looking at?" the clerk asked Chase.

"About eight hundred."

"Eight hundred and thirty-two," Jolyn answered, her head bent as she continued studying tile samples.

"Baseboard?" the clerk again asked Chase.

"Um…yeah."

"Vinyl. Two thousand thirty-seven lineal feet," Jolyn again answered. "Where are those samples?"

The clerk produced the vinyl base samples then started to ask Chase a third question. Before he got two words out, Jolyn interrupted.

"What's your installation schedule? We'll be ready for the flooring in ten days. Two weeks, tops."

The clerk's gaze went from Jolyn and Mandy to Chase, where it remained.

He shrugged. "Don't look at me. She's the contractor."

"Oh." The clerk stuttered once, recovered quickly and launched into conversation with Jolyn.

Chase half listened, wondering how often Jolyn was

mistaken for the customer rather than the contractor and if it ever bothered her.

They finished up in flooring, then visited the paint, window, plumbing, lighting and cabinet sections. When Chase would have just picked the first thing to strike his fancy, Jolyn carefully guided his choices. He would have gladly turned over the whole process to her, but it was clear she considered it her duty to involve him and, to a lesser degree, Mandy.

At least his daughter wasn't bored anymore.

Chase and Mandy waited near the door while Jolyn checked out. He insisted on pushing the cart to her truck and loading everything. Mandy asked about each item, and Jolyn patiently explained how pipe couplings fit together, what a trowel was used for and why insulation was pink.

Not long after, Jolyn steered the truck into the minimall parking lot. "What time does your movie start?"

"Thirty minutes." Chase figured he'd doze through most of the animated princess feature Mandy had begged him to see. "We should be done by five-thirty. Will that give you enough time?"

"Plenty."

She dropped them off at the curb. Chase took one gander at the length of the line outside the theater and the vast number of excited little girls and groaned. Dozing during the movie might be harder than he thought.

"Come on, Daddy." Now it was Mandy's turn to take him by the hand and drag him along to the ticket window.

While they waited their turn in line, Chase watched Jolyn drive across the parking lot. Her truck was easy to spot with its ladder racks and toolboxes. She didn't go far. Pulling out into traffic, she drove across the street and into Pineville Medical Complex parking lot.

Even after the opening credits to the movie were rolling, Chase was still wondering about the nature of Jolyn's personal errand.

"MEET ME IN MY OFFICE, Ms. Sutherland, when you're finished dressing."

Dr. Hamilton's expression was carefully schooled and gave away nothing. His equally unreadable nurse followed him out of the examination room, leaving Jolyn alone.

Tossing the paper sheet she'd worn into the hamper, she struggled into her jeans, socks and shoes, the process made difficult by her throbbing knee. Sitting for even the short period of time it had taken Dr. Hamilton to conduct his examination left her afflicted joint stiff and aching. She wasn't looking forward to the hour-long drive home.

He was seated at his desk and waiting for her when she entered his office. "I'd like you to have a CAT scan done on your knee as soon as possible."

Apparently, he wasn't one to mince words.

Dr. Hamilton was one of two orthopedic surgeons in a town too small to support many specialists and, according to Jolyn's research, the best available. She'd arranged to have her records transferred to him last week.

"Is something wrong?" A stab of worry pricked her middle. Until now, she'd assumed her pain was the result of overdoing it.

"Perhaps." He handed her a sheet of paper. "A CAT scan will help identify any problems."

Jolyn glanced down at the paper. It was a referral to an imaging center located in the same building, one floor up.

"They won't be able to take you without an appointment or I'd send you there today," Dr. Hamilton continued, his pen scratching across a small pad. "Perhaps you can stop by on your way out and make one. The sooner the better. In the meantime, here's a prescription to relieve some of the discomfort."

"I don't want anything that will make me sleepy. I have too much to do over the next few weeks not to be fully alert."

"Then you also have too much to do to be laid up, which is where you're heading if you don't take it a little easier."

Dr. Hamilton didn't sugarcoat things, either.

"Look," he said, his demeanor softening, "the CAT scan is just a precaution. I don't believe you've damaged your knee, not permanently and not yet. But you will if you aren't more careful." He passed her the prescription order. "Rest as much as possible. And keep your leg elevated. An ice pack every three hours wouldn't hurt, either. I'll call you when I get the results of the CAT scan."

He was right, of course, much as Jolyn hated to admit it. She'd been pushing herself too hard and too long.

"I'd also like you to start seeing a physical therapist three times a week."

Jolyn's jaw dropped open. "I can't make the drive that many times. I have a business to run."

"Your knee won't get better on its own."

"I know." Panic rose inside her. "Is there something I can do at home? I remember a lot of the exercises my last therapist taught me."

He frowned. "You really should work with a professional."

"What about a nurse?" Susan Raintree's daughter-in-law, Aubrey, ran the local clinic. Surely she had experience with physical therapy.

Dr. Hamilton relented, though hesitantly. "I suppose, if that's our only choice."

They discussed details for another five minutes. Jolyn promised to have Aubrey call Dr. Hamilton right away.

A small pharmacy was located on the first floor. Jolyn decided to stop there and have her prescription filled after heading upstairs to the imaging center and making her appointment.

Stepping off the elevator onto the third floor, she briefly studied the directory before turning left. A door near the end of the hallway opened and a middle-aged couple emerged. Jolyn didn't pay much attention to them until they were ten or twelve feet in front of her. At that point she glanced up… and stopped dead in her tracks.

So did they.

"Mom! Dad! What are you doing here?"

WATER BUBBLED from the center of the indoor fountain and tumbled down in musical, glistening columns. On the tiled bed of the fountain, a blanket of coins glittered and shimmered. Each one, Jolyn imagined, represented a wish. Given the fountain's location in the lobby of a medical center, those wishes were probably for good health or a speedy recovery.

"The mammogram was just routine," Jolyn's mother said from beside her. They sat on a concrete bench facing the fountain. Her father had taken Jolyn's prescription into the pharmacy to have it filled. "When a woman reaches my age, she's supposed to have one every year."

"I thought you just had one in October."

Her mother's smile was a little too bright and a little too forced. "No. It was last spring."

That was a lie, but Jolyn didn't call her mother on it. She remembered her parents coming out to visit her in Dallas during her third surgery and her mother talking about a recent checkup—complaining, really, about how the older she got, the more tests her doctor insisted on having done. A mammogram was one of the many irksome tests she'd mentioned.

"Why didn't you tell me you were having it done today?" Jolyn asked.

"I guess I forgot. It's really no big deal." Her mother turned her smile up another notch. "Why didn't you tell me about *your* doctor visit and that your knee is so bad?"

Turnabout, Jolyn supposed, was fair play. "I didn't want you to worry."

"Oh." Her mother's smile lost its luster. "And I would have."

"Like me. Like I would have worried if I'd known you were having a mammogram that wasn't part of your regular checkup."

Jolyn waited for her mother to contradict her. She merely stared into space. On the other side of the fountain, people came and went on their way in and out of the medical center, a few in wheelchairs or on crutches.

"I also didn't tell you because I knew you'd nag me not to work so hard and to take better care of myself."

"You're right about that," her mother agreed.

"Do I have the rest of it right, too?" Jolyn placed a hand on her mother's.

"I don't know what you mean."

"You didn't tell me about the mammogram because I've got enough on my plate already and you didn't want to add to it."

Her mother said nothing, which was an answer in itself and cause for concern.

"I'm surprised Dad didn't say anything."

"He didn't know about my appointment until the other day."

Concern, hell. Fear caused Jolyn's chest to tighten. If her mother had also kept her father in the dark, then whatever was wrong must be serious.

"Mom." She curled her fingers around her mother's and squeezed. "Please, tell me."

Her mother went quiet again.

"Dottie." Jolyn's father came up behind them. He handed Jolyn the bag containing her prescription and then rested his hand on his wife's shoulder. "Don't you think it's time you came clean?"

She remained stubborn for only a few seconds longer, then succumbed to the pressure. "I found some lumps in my breasts."

Jolyn swallowed. "Lumps?" The word came out rough and strange, as if her voice belonged to someone else.

"Three."

"What…um…treatment did the doctor recommend?"

"That will depend on the results of the mammogram. The lumps may not be cancer."

Cancer. Jolyn willed herself to relax, for her mother's sake more than hers. "When…when did you discover the lumps?"

"A few weeks ago, give or take."

"And you're just now having a mammogram?"

"I didn't go to the doctor right away."

"Why not, for crying out loud?"

"You were coming home, and I didn't want to—"

"Good Lord, Mom! That was over a month ago!"

Dottie sniffed and wiped her nose. "Please don't be upset with me."

Jolyn was instantly contrite. "I'm sorry. I shouldn't have raised my voice."

"You're worried." Her father left her mother's side and sat on the adjoining bench. "We both are."

"Does Steven know?"

"Not yet. And don't you tell him, either."

Jolyn would respect her mother's wishes, but grudgingly.

All at once she understood. Her mother's recent moodiness, her desire to be a bigger part of Jolyn's life, her renewed pressuring of Chase to have the DNA testing done, were prompted by a fear of having breast cancer.

She couldn't blame her mother. If Jolyn thought she had a potentially life-threatening disease, she, too, might start acting oddly or even unreasonably at times.

A young woman pushing a wailing baby in a stroller passed them.

"Maybe we should go someplace else," her father suggested in a gentle voice. "This isn't the best place to talk."

Jolyn glanced at her watch and gave a low groan. Five-forty. "I have to go. Chase and Mandy came with me and are waiting at the minimall."

"That's right. You mentioned it yesterday."

But not my doctor's appointment, Jolyn silently admonished herself.

She could hardly be angry at her mother for her being secretive when she herself was guilty of the same thing.

"Let's all sit down after dinner," her father suggested. "When we can relax."

"I think that's a good idea," her mother said.

"I'll be late." Jolyn subconsciously rubbed her knee, responsibility weighing heavily on her. "I have to take Chase and Mandy home and unload all the material I bought."

"Can't that wait until tomorrow?"

"Maybe. I don't know." If she let the chore go until the morning, she'd have that much more to do in a day that was already busy. "I guess I could pay one of the laborers to do it."

Jolyn found it hard to think. She was tired, in pain and struggling to come to terms with her mother's startling news. Standing required effort. She slowly straightened her aching leg and adjusted the shoulder bag she used for both a briefcase and a purse. The three of them moved away from the fountain.

"Wait!"

On impulse, Jolyn reached into her bag and rooted around on the bottom for a coin. When she found one, she closed her eyes and tossed it into the fountain.

Her wish made a small splash, then floated to the colorful tile bottom where it joined all the other wishes.

Chapter Six

"You want to come in for a few minutes?"

Chase's offer was so sincere, and so sweet, Jolyn had a hard time saying no. "Thanks, but I can't. My parents are waiting dinner on me."

And after dinner, they'd discuss her mother's...health concern.

"You okay?"

He'd obviously picked up on her glum mood, which would have been impossible to miss. She'd hardly spoken on the drive home.

"I'm fine. Just tired." And she was. Physically, mentally and emotionally. While she did want to talk with her parents—needed to talk to them—she wasn't altogether sure she was up to it.

Dusk had begun to fall about the same time they reached the outskirts of Blue Ridge. Indigo shadows cast by the nearby mountains—the same ones that gave the town its name—blanketed the ground, giving Chase's house a sleepy, almost surreal look. Just enough light remained for them to see that the carpenters had finished the exterior framing.

"Look!" Mandy exclaimed from the backseat. "There are walls."

Jolyn came to a stop near the back door.

"Pull around to the clinic," Chase said, "and I'll unload the material you bought."

"That isn't necessary. I'll do it in the morning. Or have one of the guys."

"Let me help."

"Chase."

His response was to hunker down in the passenger seat and stretch out his long legs.

"Daddy. Can I call 'Lizabeth and tell her about the movie?" Mandy pulled on the door handle, readying her escape.

"Sure, honey. Take your time. I'm going help Jolyn unload."

Three seconds later, the truck door slammed shut behind Mandy. Chase still hadn't moved.

"Fine." Jolyn had witnessed the infamous Raintree stubborn streak before and knew there was no use fighting it.

Pressing down on the gas pedal, she eased the truck toward the clinic, then turned around and backed up to an opening in the walls, which would eventually become the clinic's front entrance.

"Where do you want this?" Chase easily lifted a box of nails from the bed of the truck that Jolyn would have never been able to carry by herself.

"Over there." She trailed after him, a bundle of insulation under each arm. "In your surgery."

"My surgery," Chase repeated. With a satisfied smile.

Jolyn watched through the open framework as he set the box of nails down on the concrete next to a stack of two-by-fours and surveyed his surroundings.

"Maybe when we're done you can give me the grand tour."

Her resistance wavered. "All right."

She convinced herself her reasons were purely professional. A client had just asked to walk the job site with her, and she had an obligation to show it to him.

In reality, she didn't want to go home. Not yet.

They made quick work of unloading. It was almost too dark to see when Jolyn took Chase from room to room, explaining what had been done and what would be done over the coming days.

"I'm impressed," Chase said as they entered the large walk-in supply room.

"Thanks." Jolyn was proud of the clinic and the way it was coming together.

"It's bigger than it looked on paper."

"That's only because the walls aren't finished. Once the drywall goes up, the rooms will shrink."

She caught sight of a crumpled paper sack in the corner, leftover trash from somebody's lunch. Annoyed, she stooped to pick it up. She maintained a strict policy about keeping the construction site clean, especially this one as it was someone's home.

Snatching up the paper sack, she straightened and twisted sideways. Pain—needle sharp and unexpected—exploded in her knee. Without meaning to, she cried out and would have lost her balance if not for Chase.

He caught her by the elbow before she fell. When that didn't stop her forward momentum, he wrapped an arm around her waist and hauled her against him.

"Are you all right?"

"I d-don't know," she stammered, slightly breathless and hurting too much to lie. What she wouldn't give for one of those pain pills the doctor had prescribed right about now. "Just give me a minute."

"Take all the time you want." He tightened his hold on her.

Slowly, the pain lessened. Embarrassment filled the wake it left behind.

"I'm sorry," she said, feeling even worse when she realized her hands were gripping Chase's shirtfront. She loosened her fingers and attempted to disengage herself.

He would have none of it.

"Not so fast." His head dipped and his lips brushed the top of her hair.

Jolyn's heart began to pound. How long had she wanted to find herself in this exact position, locked firmly in Chase's embrace, their bodies perfectly aligned?

"I'm fine." She wasn't, and not just because of her knee, but he didn't need to know that. "You can let me go now."

"What if I don't want to?" He shifted and pressed his cheek to her temple.

Oh, God! He was going to kiss her. Bad idea. Really bad. For so many reasons.

She placed her hands on his arms and gave a gentle push. "Chase, you can't."

"Can't what? Walk you to your truck?"

If Jolyn's knee didn't still throb like the dickens, she'd kick herself. He wasn't going to kiss her. And she couldn't feel like a bigger fool.

"Or do you mean this?" he asked.

His lips sought hers, settled into place and very quickly took control, parting hers with an expertise he'd lacked in high school. Her reluctance lasted about two seconds before she succumbed with a sigh that slipped out of its own volition.

Much, much better than any painkiller.

Jolyn forgot all about her knee, about everything except the sweetly sensual liberties Chase's tongue took with her mouth, and the exquisite pressure of his palms on the small of her back. Her arms slid up to circle his neck and pulled him deeper into the kiss. He responded with a hungry moan that echoed her own rising need.

She could blame surprise for her complete lack of restraint but, in truth, she'd thought about kissing Chase often since her return. Had he not made the first move, she would never have acted on those fantasies. Certainly not while she was working for him and her mother was trying to—

Her mother! Everything about the last two hours came back to Jolyn in an emotionally jarring rush. The lumps in her mother's breasts, the imaging center, their conversation at the fountain.

Chase must have sensed her abrupt mood shift, for he ended the kiss, though with obvious reluctance. "I probably shouldn't have done that."

"I probably shouldn't have let you." She withdrew her arms and lowered her gaze, attempting to put a little emotional distance between them.

"I'm not sorry I kissed you, only that I've made you uncomfortable." He released her except for a hand on her waist.

Good thing. Jolyn had yet to regain her balance. "It's not what you think."

"Then you liked kissing me?"

His gentle teasing, so reminiscent of their long-standing friendship, gave her the courage to look at him. The smile in his voice was reflected in his dark brown eyes, which were fastened squarely on her.

She, too, tried to lighten the mood. "You have to ask?"

"My confidence has taken a beating in recent years."

"Trust me, low confidence isn't one of your problems." Clearing her throat, she moved away from Chase on legs that felt only marginally rubbery. "The timing's not right."

"What about when the timing *is* right?" They walked through the lattice of framed walls, emerging near where her truck was parked. "I won't be your client in another month."

"It's not that simple. There's a bigger obstacle than you being my client."

"Your mother," he said evenly.

Jolyn suspected he was keeping his anger in check for her benefit.

"Yes." Even if she could begin to explain, she had no right. Her mother's health was a private matter and would remain so until her mother chose to make it public. "The timing may never be right for us."

"I disagree."

He opened her truck door when she would have done it herself and helped her hop up into the cab.

"She has to give up eventually." He stood near her, just inside the open truck door. "She has no legal claim to Mandy, and no legal recourse, either."

The tone of his voice made Jolyn think he was more than prepared to stop her mother if she didn't back off soon.

"I really hope she does give up." The pain Jolyn had forgotten about returned with a vengeance as she settled behind the steering wheel and fastened her seat belt. Without thinking, she reached down and rubbed her knee.

"You should get home and put some ice on that." Chase reached up and nudged her fingers aside. Warm currents flowed through her leg as he massaged her inflamed knee. Jolyn watched, unable to tear her gaze away. His hands were strong, yet at the same time, sensitive and nimble. He knew precisely how much pressure to apply and where. She closed her eyes for a few moments and gave herself over to the sensation.

"Better?" he asked.

"Yes," she said. Her heart still ached, though. Chase had no idea how much she wished things were different, that she were free to have a romantic relationship with him.

"Our friendship is important to me. I hope I didn't screw it up tonight."

"You didn't."

The unspoken words—*I hope your mother doesn't screw it up, either*—lay between them.

"See you in the morning."

"Bright and early." Jolyn turned the key and started the engine.

"Try and get some rest tonight."

She nodded, thinking it was unlikely. If the conversation she was about to have with her parents didn't keep her up all night, reliving Chase's kiss over and over definitely would.

"THANK YOU SO MUCH, Dr. Raintree, for seeing me again."

Anita Vasquez, a young woman Chase was considering hiring as his new assistant, pumped his hand with unabashed enthusiasm.

"Call me Chase."

"Okay," she gushed, finally relinquishing her hold on him.

Her sunny smile was infectious. Chase felt the corners of his own mouth lifting for the first time since Jolyn had driven away the night before.

Where was she anyway? She said she'd be here bright and early. According to his watch, it was two hours past bright and early. In ten minutes he was due to leave for his first call of the day. Old Mr. Parkerson didn't like to be kept waiting, and would give Chase an earful if he arrived late. On the other hand, the octogenarian's cat would be more than happy about a delay. Snicker Doodle didn't like shots and let Chase know it.

At the sound of spinning tires on gravel, he glanced up. A truck—not Jolyn's—rumbled down the driveway. More workers. They'd been arriving with regular frequency since daybreak. Electricians, plumbers and Sheetrock hangers, according to the names painted on the sides of their vehicles.

"Did you get the references I e-mailed?" Anita asked.

"Yeah, I did. Dean of the college, huh? And the owner of Harvester Racing Stables?"

Anita's enormous smile turned into a grimace. "Gosh, I hope I didn't overdo it."

"No." Chase might have laughed if his nerves weren't ready to snap.

"That's good." She released a huge sigh. "Because I really want this job."

A mere slip of a girl with waist-length black hair pulled into a neat braid, Anita had put herself through veterinary school by working part-time as a jockey at Turf Paradise Race Track in Phoenix.

Her one drawback was her diminutive size. He'd have enough trouble getting the ranchers in the area to accept a woman vet. Convincing them to welcome one who needed to stand on a stool while palpating a pregnant mare might be asking the impossible.

But something about Anita appealed to Chase. Perhaps it was her determination to succeed at a job more frequently held by a man. It reminded him of Jolyn.

Where was she?

He hadn't planned on kissing her last night, should have predicted it wouldn't end well. But once he touched her, wrapped his arm around her, he couldn't help himself. Any hope of regaining his senses had died the second she parted her lips and locked her arms around his neck.

For one fantastic minute, she'd responded in ways that far exceeded his imagination—and his imagination had been going pretty far afield lately whenever he thought of her.

Chase pushed aside thoughts of last night and concentrated on the present. Mixing business with pleasure, he reminded himself, too often went awry. Her construction company and building his clinic were too important to her for him to endanger it by rushing a relationship.

When the job was done, however, all bets were off. And that included Dottie Sutherland. If Jolyn cared for him, too, and he was convinced she did—she couldn't have kissed him like she had and not care at least a little—they'd figure out what to do about her mother.

Mike Flannigan, an old friend of theirs Jolyn had hired, walked past Chase and Anita, a bulky coil of phone cable slung over his shoulder.

"Excuse me," Chase said to Anita, then hollered, "Hey, Mike. Do you know where Jolyn is this morning?"

"She called a while ago. Said she was stopping by Cutter's Market first."

"Thanks."

Good. No reason to worry. Jolyn wasn't angry or upset or avoiding him. She'd picked up material the previous day in Pineville for her new office and was dropping it off before heading to his place.

"Dr. Raintree…er, I mean Chase." Anita's enormous smile blossomed anew. "Not to be pushy or anything, but I'm available to start right away and can relocate."

He turned his full attention to her. "You free the rest of today?"

"Are you offering me the job?" Her eyes went wide.

"I'm giving you a test run. I have to be at a patient's home in…" Chase checked his watch. "Damn, I should have left five minutes ago."

"What kind of call?" Her demeanor changed to all business as they walked to Chase's truck parked near the barn.

"Feline vaccinations. Then to the Double S Ranch to oversee the semen collection and cow insemination."

"Okay." She didn't appear the least bit daunted.

"Their prize-winning bull, Peaches, is a Brahma and two thousand pounds of hunka hunka burning love. Think you can handle him?"

"Haven't met a guy yet who can resist my charms."

Chase believed her.

To reach the Double S Ranch, they had to drive through the center of town. When Chase didn't see Jolyn's truck parked outside Cutter's Market, he made the excuse of refilling his Thermos and went inside for fresh coffee. According to Mrs. Cutter, Jolyn wasn't there and hadn't been for two days, though she was expecting her soon.

His earlier agitation returned tenfold. Had he misjudged Jolyn? Was she upset about the kiss and avoiding him? Whatever it took, however many appointments he had to re-schedule, he'd see her today and apologize.

Chase wanted more than a platonic relationship with Jolyn. But he'd happily settle for that rather than lose her al-together.

THE KITCHEN DOOR shut behind Jolyn's father, leaving her and her mother alone.

"I have to get to work, too, Mom." She scooted back from the table and reached for the breakfast dishes. "I'm late."

Both Jolyn and her parents had slept in because they'd stayed up late the previous night. More than once, tears were shed, reassurances repeated, prayers offered and hands squeezed until they were numb. In the end, they'd agreed to remain calm and assume the best until Dottie's test results came back in the next day or two.

When Jolyn would have risen from her chair, her mother's hand stayed her. "There's something I need to ask you before you leave."

"Okay." The trace of desperation in her mother's voice, coupled with the tight grip on her wrist, alarmed Jolyn. This was no pick-up-some-bread-at-the-market favor.

Dottie didn't speak right away, and Jolyn's worry increased with each passing second.

"Mom?" she prompted.

Her mother visibly collected herself. "You and Chase have been spending a lot of time together recently."

Memories of their kiss returned, setting loose a flurry of tiny whirlwinds in Jolyn's stomach. She swallowed and hoped her mother didn't notice anything out of the ordinary. "I'm building his clinic and office."

"Yes, but it's more than that. You're close and growing closer."

"We're friends," she said, perhaps a bit too quickly. She need only close her eyes, and she could feel his lips, molding to fit hers and moving in ways that were definitely more than friendly.

"Yes." Dottie spoke slowly, as if picking her words with utmost care. "And because you're friends, he might be more receptive if you asked him."

Jolyn tensed. "Asked him what?"

"If he knows who Mandy's real father is."

She gnawed her lower lip, wishing her mother would let the matter of Mandy's parentage rest until they had more information on her condition.

"Hear me out before you say no."

"You can't expect me to—"

"Please."

Stark terror shone in her mother's eyes. It hit Jolyn so hard, the hair on her arms stood straight up. Her mother was scared of dying. Really and truly scared. Jolyn hadn't fully comprehended the depth of that terror until now. She'd been too busy trying to minimize it.

"All right." She settled uneasily into her seat. "I'll listen."

Her mother visibly collected herself before continuing. "I think Chase knows Steven is Mandy's real father and that's why he refuses to have the DNA testing done."

"He could also know *he's* her real father."

"If that's true, why doesn't he have the testing done? It would be the simplest solution and get me off his back once and for all."

"Because he doesn't have to."

Or, Jolyn thought, he was afraid of the findings. With her next breath, her heart went out to him. How hard it must be for him to struggle with the constant uncertainty, if he was indeed uncertain.

"I'd like you to ask him for me."

"If he knows Steven is Mandy's real father?"

"Yes."

"I would never do that to him." Jolyn crossed her arms over her middle. "Even if I could bring myself to ask him, what makes you think he'd tell me?"

"He might. Especially if you played on his sympathies."

"You're suggesting I tell him about the lumps in your breasts?"

"Absolutely not." Her mother looked aghast.

"Then what?"

"Say it's important for *you* to know if Mandy's your niece or not. Don't mention me."

"Lie to him, you mean."

"You wouldn't be lying exactly."

"I wouldn't be telling the truth, either."

"I realize I'm putting you on the spot." Dottie meticulously folded and refolded her paper napkin into a small square as she talked. "Will you at least reconsider if it turns out I have... If my mammogram...shows something?"

The panic in her mother's eyes had been replaced by a desperation that begged Jolyn to understand. Her rock-solid conviction crumbled a little. "I don't know...."

"Put yourself in my place. How would you feel if you thought you might die?"

How *would* she feel? Scared out of her mind, naturally. Worried about the family she was leaving behind. And she'd want to spend whatever time she had left with those she loved. Her husband, if she had one, and children. *Grandchildren.*

Oh, God.

What if Mandy really was Steven's daughter and not

Chase's? Was it fair that her mother be deprived of her grand-daughter in the last days of her life?

Stop thinking like that, Jolyn told herself. *Your mother is not going to die.*

"I don't like taking advantage of Chase's and my friendship."

"He could be more," Dottie offered quietly. "If that's what you want."

Was it?

Jolyn recalled the wild, wonderfully satisfying sensations she'd experienced in his arms.

Was it possible? Could she and Chase date? Jolyn was so used to thinking of him as "off-limits," thinking of him as "available" didn't come easy. She forced herself to consider the possibilities and immediately warmed to them. Once the clinic was finished, nothing prevented them from dating.

"I think you and Chase would be good for each other."

Something in her mother's tone gave Jolyn pause. "Why do you say that?"

"You have a lot in common."

"Like a stake in who Mandy's real father is?" Jolyn hated to admit she doubted her mother's motives.

"I was referring to your love of horses."

"Oh." Maybe she'd been wrong.

Or had she?

If she and Chase did start dating, her mother would have a built-in excuse to get close to Mandy. And what if she took advantage of the opportunity? Would Chase then think Jolyn had tricked him? The idea that a moment ago had appealed to her suddenly left a bad taste in her mouth.

She was shortsighted, if not foolish, to think she and Chase could enjoy a complication-free romantic relationship. Certainly not while her mother was sick.

Steering the conversation away from her and Chase, Jolyn said, "I still think you should talk to Steven. You can't acknowledge Mandy as your granddaughter without him having to acknowledge her as his daughter."

"He'll support me."

"He hasn't before now."

"Circumstances are different."

There was that reminder again, the black cancer cloud hanging over their heads.

"You've told him about the lumps then?"

"No. And don't you, either."

"He has a right to know."

"I'll tell him," her mother said. "Eventually."

The catch in Dottie's voice affected Jolyn deeply. Perhaps she'd been wrong to doubt her mother's motive. She might want nothing more than to see her daughter happy.

"You're going to live to be a hundred, Mom. Your doctor said the lumps could be cysts or benign tumors or any of a dozen harmless abnormalities."

"You didn't see his face. It wasn't that of a doctor who suspected harmless abnormalities."

"He's simply being cautious." Jolyn had plenty of experience with doctors and knew them to be reserved when offering opinions. Placing a hand atop her mother's, something she was doing a lot of since yesterday, she said, "I really need to get to work. We'll talk more tonight when I get home."

She'd been ignoring the hundred and one tasks awaiting her at Chase's and Cutter's Market. There were times when family came first, and this was definitely one of them. But that didn't eliminate her other responsibilities.

Mike had recently taken on some superintendent duties, and she hoped like heck he could handle work on the clinic until she arrived, which, at the rate her morning was progressing, would be nine-thirty or ten. She made a mental note to call him the second she got into her truck.

"Please think about what I've said," her mother implored. "And try to see my side."

"I will." She'd find it hard to think of anything else.

In the next second, the kitchen phone rang.

Her mother jumped out of her chair, then purposefully slowed her steps as she strode to the counter where the portable phone lay. "Probably one of my students' mothers."

It was clear from Dottie's white-knuckled grip on the receiver she wasn't talking to a student's mother. Jolyn's insides turned to ice.

"That was my doctor's office." With shaking hands, her mother set down the phone and pulled the flaps of her robe tight, wrapping herself in a flannel cocoon. "He wants to see me for a consultation right away. Monday if possible."

Chapter Seven

"Well, there you are." Mrs. Cutter squeezed into the market's minuscule restroom where Jolyn sat on the closed toilet lid facing backward, her arm inside the tank. Spread out on the floor beside her feet was a pile of parts, both old and new. "Everybody's been looking for you today."

"Who's everybody?"

"The Buchanans came by about a half hour ago."

"Don't think I know them." Jolyn only half listened. Her mind was still on her mother and the call from her doctor's office.

"Weekenders. They moved here two summers back. Nice enough people, I reckon." In Mrs. Cutter-speak, "nice enough" was a high compliment. "They're wantin' to enclose their back porch." She switched the plastic straw she habitually chewed on to the opposite side of her mouth and rolled her eyes. "Build one of them solariums with plants and skylights."

"Really?"

"I gave 'em your flyer. They asked me to have you call 'em."

Enclosing a porch and building a solarium wasn't on the same scale as a vet clinic and office, but at this stage in her business, Jolyn couldn't afford to be picky.

"Did you get their phone number?" she asked.

"Do I look like your secretary?"

"No." Jolyn flushed the toilet, glad to see the tank empty of water with a sloshy gurgle and not overflow as it had been doing.

"'Course I got their phone number." Mrs. Cutter stood behind Jolyn, peering over her shoulder. She grunted with satisfaction when the tank began to quickly refill. "It's up at the register."

"Thank you. I'll come get it when I'm done with the repairs."

"Chase was in here looking for you earlier, too. I didn't get his phone number. Reckon you already have it."

Jolyn chided herself for not calling and letting him know she was running late. So much for promoting customer relations.

"Had some young gal with him."

"Oh?"

By "young gal," Mrs. Cutter meant a stranger. In a small town like Blue Ridge, new people gathered a lot of attention.

"Told me he was considering hiring her as his assistant."

Jolyn swung around to face forward and began collecting the old, worn-out toilet parts. She stuffed them into the same plastic sack the new parts had come in and shut the lid on her toolbox.

"That's good. He needs an assistant."

"This one didn't look like she'd even graduated kindergarten yet. Old Mrs. Shaughnessy will tear her teeny tiny hide in two."

"Is that where they were heading? Up to the Double S?"

"Yep. Just leave that." Mrs. Cutter shooed Jolyn aside when she attempted to wipe up the floor where water had spilled. "I'll get it."

"You sure?"

"I know you got work to do. Paying work. Get after it." She preceded Jolyn out of the restroom and into the crowded, twisting hall with its towers of boxes, crates and cartons. "When you gonna put that poor boy outta his misery?"

"What poor boy?"

Jolyn's feigned naivety earned her yet another eye roll from Mrs. Cutter. "Gawd bless. Chase, 'a course. He's got it bad for you."

"We're just friends." Jolyn wondered how often she would repeat that phrase today.

"Friends don't wear no kicked-puppy sad faces when their girl ain't where they expect her to be."

Mrs. Cutter must not have noticed that Jolyn stopped cold in her tracks. She went through the door and into the store, leaving Jolyn alone.

Chase really *was* interested in her. Romantically, sexually, and…wow! Yes, there had been the kiss and the discussion about timing not being right, but Jolyn had so far only thought about their evolving relationship from her own perspective.

What now? Go to him? No, he was at the Double S Ranch. Wait for him then at his house?

Her heart gave a small leap at the thought of seeing him, followed closely by a wave of insecurity. What should she say to him?

Her shoulders sagged. She'd say nothing for now, not until her mother visited her doctor.

What a fix to find herself in. The guy she'd secretly carried a torch for all through high school was finally free to date her, finally returning her feelings, and she couldn't do anything about it.

"Where'd you go?" Mrs. Cutter stuck her head around the corner.

Jolyn straightened. "Sorry."

"You okay?"

"Yeah." She walked toward the door, trying to act as if her world was all roses and sunshine. "Just thinking about work."

"Everything okay at home?" Mrs. Cutter's usual scratchiness gave way to thoughtful concern.

"Fine," Jolyn said, perhaps a tad too quickly.

"I only ask cuz when I went by the post office this morning, your dad said the same thing when I caught him standing with his back holding up the wall."

"Leaky kitchen faucet kept us up last night."

Mrs. Cutter's eagle-eye gaze narrowed into one of suspicion. "You'd think a person handy with a wrench like you are wouldn't let that happen."

"You'd think."

Great, Jolyn grumbled to herself and shuffled through the door, balancing her heavy toolbox. If Mrs. Cutter, owner of gossip central, had figured out something was amiss in the Sutherland family, it wouldn't be long before everyone in Blue Ridge knew it, too.

DESPITE HIS EARLIER determination, three days came and went without Chase having a chance to talk to Jolyn. Usually, they were surrounded by workers. Once he caught her alone, but her mood was a bit off, as if she were preoccupied, so he kept quiet. Before he knew it, the weekend had arrived—one with no scheduled calls, thanks to Anita.

Since spending more time with his daughter was Chase's goal, he suggested an early Saturday morning ride, promising they would return well before her eleven o'clock dance lesson. Clearly, spending time together wasn't as important to Mandy as it was to him. She asked if her friend Elizabeth could go with them. He agreed, mostly because it pleased him to see his daughter happy and not moping over SherryAnne canceling her upcoming birthday visit.

Cinnamon, Mandy's exceedingly gentle, pint-sized horse, waited patiently for Chase to finish saddling her. The same couldn't be said for the girls. They giggled and played as they packed a picnic snack of juice boxes and homemade brownies in the saddlebags on Elizabeth's horse, a slightly larger, much older version of Cinnamon.

For once, the driveway was empty of construction vehicles. Jolyn had evidently taken the morning off, too, or was working at another job. Chase hoped the former. She worked too hard, and he worried about her. He hoped their kiss the other night hadn't added to her stress, which was why he wanted to talk to her.

"You two ready?"

"Almost." Mandy finished boosting Elizabeth up onto her horse.

"Don't forget to put the dogs in the garage."

Mandy scampered off, Buzz and Lickety in hot pursuit.

Chase gathered Cinnamon's reins and those of his mount, Matilda, a four-year-old Dutch warmblood mare and his current favorite. She stood nearly seventeen hands tall and had a rich chestnut coat the texture of satin.

No other horse could beat her on the trail. Strong and muscular, with boundless energy, she scaled steep, rocky slopes as if they were backyard dirt piles. Only a mile-wide stubborn streak kept her from being the best damn horse he'd ever owned.

Chase led Matilda and Cinnamon toward the house. Elizabeth brought up the rear, pushing her old gelding for a speed he didn't have in him anymore. Which was just fine with Chase. He'd have his hands full with Matilda and didn't need to be worried about the girls.

Once he and Mandy joined Elizabeth in the saddle, they headed down the driveway. At the road, Chase pulled Matilda to a stop. "Which way, ladies? Neglian Creek crossing or Uncle Joseph's and Aunt Susan's ranch?"

"Neglian Creek," both girls answered and turned their horses to the right.

Chase had to maintain a short rein on Matilda, who, given her head, would have charged out in front of the girls. The creek, however, would be a different story. Matilda didn't like water and getting her to cross it, even when it was only a few inches deep, inevitably resulted in a test of wills.

It wasn't long before Chase changed his mind and was glad the girls had chosen the Neglian Creek crossing. Not a quarter mile from the trailhead, the back end of a familiar paint horse came into view between the sprawling mixture of oak and pine trees.

Sinbad. And sitting astride him, Jolyn. She'd evidently stopped for a break where the trail split into two branches, one leading to the creek and the other up the mountain to the old Ladderback mine.

A slow smile spread across Chase's face as he watched her lift a canteen to her mouth and take a long drink. Morning sun filtered through the leafy tree branches, bathing her in alternating patches of shadow and light. The stunning combination of woman, horse and nature came together perfectly for one tiny instant.

"Look, Dad," Mandy cried. "It's Jolyn."

"So I see."

"Jolyn, Jolyn." Mandy waved and nudged Cinnamon into a trot.

"Hello." Jolyn hung her canteen over her saddle horn and waved back, her hazel eyes shining with welcome.

Chase's smile widened. Not that he hadn't been enjoying himself with his daughter and her friend, but suddenly their ride promised to be much more fun.

"Nice to see you took the day off work," he said once they were in talking distance. "You needed it."

"Only for a couple of hours." She patted Sinbad's neck. "This big fellow hasn't been ridden in a week and was ready to break down the fence. But after lunch, it's back to the grindstone."

"Your leg must be feeling better."

"It is. I started physical therapy with Aubrey, and it seems to be helping." She absently rubbed her knee.

Chase was reminded of the other night when he'd done the same thing. Something inside him stirred. As if sensing his changing mood, she abruptly stopped and adjusted her cowboy hat to fit more snugly on her head.

"Where you going?"

"Neglian Creek crossing," Mandy chimed in.

Chase hadn't seen Jolyn in anything but a ball cap since she'd come home. The cowboy hat made her look like a teenager again and much like the Jolyn he remembered. How could he have failed to notice her fresh-faced beauty all those years ago?

"What about you?" he asked.

"I was thinking of checking out the old mine."

"Why don't you come with us?" Mandy issued the invitation a split second ahead of Chase.

"We can't stay long," he added. "Mandy has to be back for her dance lesson."

"Thank you," Jolyn said softly.

"You're doing me a favor. The girls were already getting tired of my company." As if to prove his point, Mandy and Elizabeth rode ahead a bit to look at the clusters of colorful wildflowers.

"Not for that."

He gave Jolyn a quizzical look. "What then?"

"For letting Mandy continue with her lessons. You have every reason to pull her out."

"She loves dance class. And as long as your mom keeps her end of the bargain," Chase said quietly, "Mandy will continue going to class." He applied a slight pressure to Matilda's flanks and in a louder voice, said, "Let's go."

With the girls behind him and Jolyn beside him, they headed down the trail at a leisurely walk. The rhythmic clip-clop of hooves on hard-packed dirt was the only sound for several minutes.

Chase was hesitant to break the companionable lull, but he did. "I hired an assistant."

"Really?"

"It's because of her I have today off."

"Her?" Jolyn's eyebrows lifted. "Not him? You're really turning this town on its ears."

"Yeah. I figure, why break my streak? The last woman I hired seems to be working out okay. Don't you agree?"

Her smile lost its luster. Chase thought he knew why.

"About the other night… I owe you an apology."

"No, you don't," she argued.

"You are not to blame, you hear me? Don't even think it."

"I'm not. Because there's no blame to give or take." She looked him straight in the face. "I don't regret what happened."

A jolt of sexual energy ripped through Chase, hot and fierce and unlike any he'd previously experienced. "Me, neither. And I'm damn sure not averse to it happening again."

With a swiftness that surprised him, he reached across the short distance separating them to take Jolyn's hand. The horses cooperated by walking quietly, shoulder to shoulder.

She stared at their joined hands, and he felt her fingers tense.

"Not now," he said and eased his grip. "Later. When the clinic is finished. I promise not to kiss you again until then." But kiss her he would, the very day the last nail was hammered in place.

"Chase, I…"

The same preoccupation he'd noticed in her before returned. "Hey, what's wrong?" He massaged the inside of her wrist with the pad of his thumb.

"Nothing." She offered him an unconvincing smile.

At least she didn't pull away, even when Elizabeth started giggling.

He'd have liked to question Jolyn further, hold on to her

longer, but his cell phone rang. Hoping it wasn't an emergency call, he pulled the phone from the clip on his belt.

"You get reception clear out here?" she asked incredulously.

"Radio phone with a booster antenna." Chase checked the caller ID, and his pulse instantly accelerated. "Hold up, girls."

He pulled on the reins, and Matilda obediently stopped. Jolyn and Sinbad did likewise.

Few calls would be important enough to take him away from a morning ride with his daughter and Jolyn. This was one of them.

"Yeah, Chuck."

He listened intently, committing the details of where and when to meet to memory as he didn't have a pen and paper handy. Jolyn watched him intently, openly curious.

"That didn't sound like an animal emergency," she said when he disconnected and replaced his phone.

"Chuck's my platoon leader."

"Like in the army?"

"Law enforcement. I'm a member of the Blue Ridge mounted sheriff's posse. We've been called on a search and rescue."

"For what?"

"Not what. Who. An eighteen-year-old boy. He and his buddies were hiking up near Saddle Horn Butte yesterday. The other boys made it back this morning. He got separated last night and is still missing."

"Oh, my God! That's terrible."

"I have to meet up with my platoon at the base of the mountain in two hours." He swung Matilda around and pointed her back the way they came. "Girls." He beckoned them with a wave. "We have to go home."

"Why?" Mandy complained with a pout.

Elizabeth appeared equally crestfallen.

"Not now, sweetie." Chase's tone was firm. "I don't have the time."

"How 'bout I take the girls to Neglian Creek crossing?" Jolyn said. "I'll make sure Mandy gets to her dance lesson on time."

"I can't impose on you like that."

"I insist." Her tone was as firm as his.

"Oh, Daddy. Can we please stay with Jolyn?" Mandy's bright green eyes pleaded with him.

He hesitated for an instant, then relented. Every minute counted when a person was missing in the wilderness, and he had a lot to do to get ready. With Jolyn's help, he'd be done that much sooner.

"I'll call Mrs. Payne when I get to the house," he said. "She'll pick up Mandy after dance class and take her to my aunt and uncle's house. And I'll let Elizabeth's mother know what's going on."

"Don't worry," Jolyn said. "We'll manage."

"I'll be in touch when I can. But don't worry if that isn't until tomorrow. We could be out all night."

"Just find that boy."

"You listen to Jolyn, you hear me?" He emphasized his warning to Mandy by leveling a finger at her. "Whatever she says, you do it."

Both girls nodded solemnly but from the neck down, they fidgeted with excitement.

"Thanks," he told Jolyn, wishing he hadn't made that promise about not kissing her.

Confident that his daughter and her friend were in good hands, Chase gave Matilda her head and raced home at a full gallop.

Chapter Eight

"Your mom and dad and I used to come here all the time when we were young." Jolyn tethered Sinbad to a low-hanging tree branch. The horse immediately lowered his head and sniffed the ground for stalks of grass.

"For picnics, like us?" Mandy asked, distributing the brownies and juice boxes.

"Most of the kids came up here to…explore." Jolyn changed her story at the last second. She wasn't about to tell the girls what the local teenagers did—and probably were still doing—at the old Ladderback mine.

They'd decided on a different destination after Chase left to join his platoon on their search-and-rescue mission. The girls went often to Neglian Creek crossing but had only been to the mine once and that was in a four-wheel-drive vehicle.

"What did you explore for?"

"Oh, the usual. Arrowheads. Secret tunnels. Buried treasure."

"Ever find any?"

Mandy and Elizabeth picked boulders on which to sit. Beside them, over a small ridge, a narrow stream splashed down the mountainside to join its much bigger cousin, Neglian Creek.

"Nope. Just lots of spiders and snakes and a big, furry

raccoon. Once, your dad went really deep into the mine and stumbled on a whole bunch of bats."

"Ew!" Elizabeth shuddered in revulsion.

Mandy was apparently made of stronger stuff. "Cool. Can you take us there?"

"Absolutely not. It isn't safe. Mike, you know him, he's helping me build your dad's clinic. When we were in high school, he fell into the shaft and broke his arm in three places."

Poor Mike had been trying to impress Jolyn when his stunt backfired. She'd visited him the next day at home and signed his cast. She'd also accepted his invitation to the school dance, mostly out of guilt. And because Chase was already going with SherryAnne.

"Your dad had to climb down and get him."

"Was Mom there, too?" Mandy perched on the edge of her boulder, listening raptly.

"Yes."

"Did she help rescue Mike?"

Jolyn didn't remember much of what SherryAnne did beyond complaining that their afternoon fun was cut short.

"Yes, a little," she said, stretching the truth for Mandy's benefit. "Mostly your dad helped. He rescued Mike from the mine and led both horses all the way back to town because Mike couldn't hold on to the reins."

"My mom and Jolyn were *best* friends," Mandy informed Elizabeth. "But my mom and dad were boyfriend and girlfriend."

"Jolyn and your dad are boyfriend and girlfriend now," Elizabeth said matter-of-factly.

"No, they're not," Mandy answered hotly.

"We're not boyfriend and girlfriend," Jolyn assured the girls.

Elizabeth was undaunted. "You were holding hands."

Mandy looked confused and unhappy.

"I was upset about something, and your dad was trying to make me feel better. We're just friends."

There was that phrase again.

The tension in Mandy's thin frame visibly lessened. She was clearly uncomfortable with the notion of her father dating, even someone she liked.

Jolyn hadn't taken the little girl's feelings into consideration when she'd contemplated having a relationship with Chase.

Perhaps she'd been fooling herself. Hurting Mandy, coming between her and her father, wasn't an option. Her mother was already doing that, or trying to.

Brushing her hands on her jeans, she stood, determined to restore the mood to what it had been when they first arrived. "Just because I won't let you go down into the mine doesn't mean we can't look inside. Who here wants to go with me?"

Mandy jumped up, all bright eyes and big smile again. "I do."

Elizabeth's enthusiasm didn't match Mandy's. "As long as there aren't any bats."

"We won't be going that far down the shaft." Jolyn planned to let the girls venture just inside the mine opening where she knew from personal experience that the ground was solid and the rafters stable. But no deeper. "Besides, bats sleep during the day."

"Is there any gold in here?" Mandy asked once they'd scaled the footpath leading to the mine's entrance.

Jolyn had gone slowly so as not to aggravate her knee. "Actually, the prospectors in these parts dug for silver, or so the stories go." She hauled Elizabeth up onto the ledge with her and Mandy.

Then all three stared into the seemingly endless pitch-black tunnel. A current of slow-moving air swirled out from the dark to glide over them, chilling their faces and arms. Jolyn had forgotten about the cold.

"It's not very big," Mandy observed.

The girls' heads barely cleared the top rafter. Jolyn would have to stoop over to enter.

"The shaft is bigger inside. But not much and only for a little ways. It gets smaller the farther back you go." Chase had had to crawl on his hands and knees to pull Mike out.

"What are these?" Mandy inched forward until she stood close enough to the rafters to run her hand over the rough and scarred wood.

"Names and dates and different graffiti kids have carved." Not to mention a few obscenities Jolyn hoped the girls didn't notice.

"Sure is a lot of them."

"About a hundred and thirty years' worth."

The modern-day hieroglyphics covered every available inch of surface space. It was a wonder that many carvings hadn't weakened the rafters to the point of collapse.

"Did you ever write your name here?" Mandy asked.

"No. But your dad did."

"Where? Show me!"

Jolyn crossed to the other side of the entrance and squatted. "Around here somewhere." In truth, she knew exactly where to locate Chase's carving, having stared at it more often than she cared to admit. "There." She indicated a pair of initials, one above the other, linked by a plus sign in the middle.

"Who's S.B.?"

"Your mother."

"Her initials are S.R."

"They are now. Back in high school, her name was SherryAnne Bakersfield."

"Oh, yeah. I forgot." Mandy stared at the initials for a long, silent moment. "My dad really loved my mom," she said, tracing the initials with the tip of her index finger.

"Of course he did. And she loved him."

"I just wish she still did." Mandy's voice rose barely above a whisper. Had Jolyn not been right beside her, she wouldn't have heard.

"What's important is that she loves *you*. And always will."

"I guess."

Mandy gazed at the initials with quiet intensity. For a second, Jolyn thought the girl might cry. And who could blame her? Even at her young age, Mandy knew an empty platitude when she heard one.

Damn SherryAnne. Canceling her visit verged on cruelty. What could be more important than celebrating a daughter's birthday? A daughter she hadn't seen in a year.

Since Mandy didn't appear keen on conversation, Jolyn opted to leave her alone for a few minutes. Elizabeth had gone back outside and was kneeling on the ground in front of the mine opening, watching parallel lines of black ants march in and out of a huge anthill.

"You like insects?" Jolyn asked. She kept one eye on Mandy, just as a precaution.

"They're kinda neat. My parents are always making me and my sisters watch *Animal World* and the Nature Channel instead of cartoons." Elizabeth made it sound like torture.

"But you don't like bats."

"Ick!" She made a face, sat back on her fanny and hollered, "Come on, Mandy. I'm bored."

"We really should leave, honey," Jolyn added, "if you want to make your dance lesson on time."

Mandy stepped out into the sunlight. She'd stopped looking like she might cry, but Jolyn could tell that she was hiding her hurt and pain. Just like Chase.

The ride home went well. All remnants of Mandy's pensive mood fled when they reached the road and Jolyn let the girls lope their horses across a stretch of open meadow. By the time they stopped, they were breathing heavier than the horses—from laughter more than exertion.

"Look, there's a log." Mandy waved excitedly. "Can we jump it?"

"Is Cinnamon able to?"

"She's jumped way higher than that lots of times."

"I don't know."

"Daddy lets me."

Jolyn did recall seeing low jumps in the practice arena at Chase's house. And the log couldn't be more than two feet off the ground. She, too, had jumped her horse higher than that when she was Mandy's age.

"Well…"

"Please."

Jolyn took comfort that Cinnamon wasn't tall and the ground was covered in thick, green grass. If Elizabeth's old horse did more than walk over the log, she'd be surprised. "All right."

Mandy trotted Cinnamon toward the log. A split second before reaching it, the small horse came to a sudden stop. Then, with a snorting grunt, she popped over the log. Everybody cheered. Elizabeth's old horse had apparently jumped before because he approached the log without hesitation and easily cleared it.

"Your turn," Mandy said.

"Me? No." Jolyn shook her head. "I'm enjoying watching you two."

"You have to," the girls insisted.

Without warning, a paralyzing fear gripped Jolyn. She might have been facing an open pit of burning lava and not a fallen log in the middle of a grassy meadow. Giving herself a swift mental kick, she gripped the reins with hands slick from sweat. She hadn't jumped since the accident and wasn't remotely ready to try.

"We have to get back for your dance class."

"Not yet, we don't. Come on."

She was being ridiculous. The log was only two feet high

for crying out loud. She'd jumped three times that height during every performance in the Wild and Wooly West Equestrian Show. Always without a hitch. Except for once. And that had been a humdinger of a hitch.

Sinbad pawed the ground. He'd waited while the other horses had their turn and was now ready for his. And why not? Since the day Jolyn's parents brought him home thirteen years ago, she'd been taking him over obstacles of every shape and size. No, that wasn't entirely true. He hadn't jumped since the accident, either.

But unlike her, he couldn't wait to try again.

"Hurry," the girls chimed. "You're taking forever. It's just a log."

Yes, a log. Not a wagon filled with mock settlers. She could do this. And she might never have a better opportunity to test herself.

Sweat trickled down her neck and dampened the collar of her shirt. Air rushed from her lungs only to be drawn swiftly back. Her pulse thrummed, echoing the pounding inside her head.

Sinbad must have sensed her agitation as his pawing gave way to prancing in place. One squeeze of her legs and he'd fly like the wind.

Jolyn tugged on the reins. Sinbad instantly stopped prancing, only to collect himself.

"Go," she whispered before she lost her nerve.

When he would have run, she held him to a trot. A slow, *slow* trot. Used to clearing far larger objects, Sinbad didn't do much more than lift his front legs off the ground.

It was enough for Jolyn.

The girls clapped and for one instant, Jolyn was performing in the show again. Only then, she hadn't trembled from head to toe or felt her chest ache like she'd just run a marathon.

"We really should get a move on," she said, dragging in a

ragged breath. They still had a half-hour ride ahead of them, and Mandy needed to change for dance class.

Realizing they were going home, the horses picked up the pace.

You did it, Jolyn commended herself as they rode. *You jumped Sinbad and survived.* Though far from conquering her fear, she hadn't let it defeat her.

God willing, she wouldn't have to test herself again anytime soon.

"SUTHERLAND CONSTRUCTION?" a deep male voice called out.

"Who is it?" Jolyn stood on a stepladder, her back to the open office door, her head inside an air-conditioning duct and her fingers buried in a tangled clump of electrical wire.

"Delivery from Office Central. Someone order a desk?"

"A desk?" Jolyn dropped the wire and carefully climbed down the ladder. "I didn't order any—" She turned and let out a gasp. "Steven!" Breaking into a huge grin, she hurried across the room to throw herself in her brother's arms. She hadn't seen him since her last supply run to Pineville. "What in the world are you doing here?"

"I told you. I'm delivering a desk."

"But I—"

"Mom mentioned you needed one. And no," he pinched her chin between his thumb and forefinger, "you won't pay me back. Consider it an office-warming present."

"Oh, Steven. I can't accept." Her brother worked as a manager for a family-style restaurant in Pineville. He was doing okay financially, but he and his girlfriend had recently purchased a new house and new furniture to go with it.

"Don't refuse until you've seen it. We're not talking top of the line here."

"Thank you." Framing his face with her hands, she pulled him down and kissed his forehead. She'd return the favor one day soon by doing some landscaping or upgrades on the house for him and Bethany.

He studied her critically before releasing her. "You look tired."

"I am, a little."

"How's the knee? Mom said it was bothering you."

"Did she now?" Jolyn asked raising an eyebrow. Evidently their mother saw fit to mention Jolyn's minor medical complaint but not her own major one.

That might change after today. Her parents were at that moment en route to visit her mother's doctor in Pineville. Jolyn's offer to accompany them had been refused. Rather than drive herself crazy playing "what-if" all afternoon, she decided to tackle some of the renovations at her new office.

Holding out her leg for her brother's inspection, she said, "The knee's much better, as you can see. I've been taking it easy and doing my exercises."

"You call standing on a ladder taking it easy?"

"Compared to crawling around on a rooftop, yes." She didn't mention she'd been doing precisely that an hour earlier. "I had a CAT scan done last week and the doctor said everything looks fine. I just overdid it at first."

"How's Chase's clinic coming?"

"Terrific. We're about two days ahead of schedule."

"I hope he appreciates how hard you're working."

"Actually, he doesn't know yet. About the schedule," she clarified. "He went on a search and rescue with the Blue Ridge mounted posse and didn't get home until yesterday. They found the boy. Alive and well," she added.

"That's good." Steven nodded, his features revealing nothing of what he was thinking.

Jolyn stuffed her hands in her jeans pockets. She was always careful when discussing Chase with her brother for obvious reasons. Steven was no saint and had rightfully earned his share of the blame in the affair with SherryAnne. In Jolyn's opinion, however, he'd redeemed himself somewhat by leaving Chase and SherryAnne alone and staying far away from Mandy.

If only the same could be said about their mother.

"My little sister." Steven wrapped his arm around Jolyn and gave her an enthusiastic hug. "An up-and-coming business woman. Who'd've thunk it?"

"Is that an insult or a compliment?"

"Compliment, of course." He released her, and they walked toward the door.

"Mike's doing a bang-up job as superintendent." When Jolyn left Chase's place earlier, he was riding herd on the drywall tapers.

"Mike Flannigan!" Steven's outburst rang with skepticism. "The same Mike Flannigan who got kicked out of 4-H for using permanent markers to draw naked women on Wanda Cummings's pigs right before the state fair?"

"'Fraid so." Jolyn couldn't help laughing. "He's matured a lot since high school. He's even a member of the volunteer fire department."

Steven drew back in disbelief. "This I've gotta see." Switching gears, he said, "Where do you want the desk? Be warned, it's in pieces."

"The corner, I guess. And in pieces is fine. I'll only have to move it again when I install the new carpet." Jolyn had recently torn up the old vinyl tile, leaving behind bare concrete.

"I'd say the place is coming along but…" He shrugged.

"Hey. Be nice." She cuffed him in the arm. "You think this is bad, you should have seen it before."

"Come on, String Bean. Let's unload your desk. Better yet, I'll unload and you watch. Got a handcart anywhere nearby?"

"Mrs. Cutter does in the back room. I'll ask her if we can borrow it."

Like the two children they'd once been, they bickered constantly over the desk. Steven insisted on doing everything himself, and Jolyn refused to let him, claiming *she* was the expert. In the end, it took them twice as long as it should have.

"I'm hungry," Steven announced when they were done. "What have you got to eat around here?"

"Whatever's in the store. Mrs. Cutter lets me run a tab."

"She still make those rotgut chili dogs?"

"With cheese and jalapeños?"

Steven pressed a hand to his chest and groaned. "I can feel the heartburn already."

"Two enough?"

"And an extra large Dr Pepper."

Since there were no chairs in Jolyn's office, they went outside and perched on a low block wall behind the market to enjoy their meal.

"I hear Mom's pestering Chase again to have DNA testing done."

Steven's comment, so out of the blue, took Jolyn aback. "Who told you?"

"Dad. He stopped by the restaurant one afternoon a few Saturdays back when he was in Pineville."

Before her mother's mammogram, Jolyn thought. "She is. Or was. I think she's agreed to cool it. Temporarily, anyway."

Longer, if her tests were normal. Jolyn intended to see to it. And they would be normal. Taking her own advice, she was assuming the best.

"Fine by me if she abandons the idea altogether." Steven polished off his first chili dog and took a big swig of soda before biting into the second one. "Mandy's not my daughter."

"You sound so sure."

"I am. And that's not just wishful thinking." He stopped eating and pushed a lock of shaggy blond hair off his face. In a community where most guys favored cowboy hats and silver belt buckles, Steven's rock musician looks always stood out.

"Did SherryAnne tell you you're not Mandy's father?"

"Hell, no. She didn't have to."

Jolyn's "Hmm," was rife with doubt.

"If Mandy's my kid," Steven said, "then she was born three weeks early."

"Babies are born early every day."

"Except Mandy was something like nine and a half pounds. That doesn't sound like any premature baby I've ever heard of."

"I don't remember. I was gone by then, on my first tour."

"Well, *I* remember. Mom made sure I knew about the baby because she thought I was the father."

Jolyn lost interest in her hot dog and set it aside. "But Sherry-Anne's tall for a woman. Mandy could simply take after her."

Then again, Chase was tall, too. He had three inches on her brother.

"Anyone will tell you I'm not parent material," her brother went on. "Though lately I've been thinking kids might be okay with the right woman."

"Do tell." His girlfriend, Jolyn decided, must be having a positive effect on him.

He flashed her an almost embarrassed smile before abruptly sobering. "I've only seen Mandy from a distance. But even so, wouldn't I feel something for her? Like a connection or bond? I don't, in case you're wondering," he declared, anticipating Jolyn's question.

She absently twirled the straw in her soda. "People aren't emperor penguins. I'm not sure we instinctively recognize our offspring." Jolyn didn't add that her brother might not feel a connection to Mandy because deep down, he didn't want to.

"Trust me, you're not telling me anything I haven't already thought of myself. But you've yet to mention the main reason I'm convinced Mandy's not my kid."

"What's that?"

"SherryAnne and I have spoken exactly twice since the day Chase walked in on us at their apartment in Pineville."

Jolyn chuckled mirthlessly. "That's hardly a reason. She and I have barely talked since then, either."

"Exactly," Steven exclaimed as if Jolyn had reached a brilliant conclusion. "If I were Mandy's father, SherryAnne would have come to me by now, demanding a payoff. Money's always been her top priority in life."

Jolyn was struck by the rancor in her brother's voice and the pain in his expression. Had he been in love with SherryAnne? The instant the thought occurred to Jolyn, she knew she was right. No one, herself included, had ever considered the possibility that Steven might have been hurt by what happened, only that he, like SherryAnne, had done the hurting.

"Chase was in vet school at the time." Steven stared sightlessly at the slow stream of passing traffic. "He and SherryAnne were living on whatever money his parents gave them and her wages from the Clip and Curl. I was far from rich but I did have a decent job and made more than the two of them put together. SherryAnne would have jumped Chase's ship for mine in a heartbeat if Mandy was my kid."

"Is that want you hoped?" Jolyn asked gently.

Steven's startled look confirmed her suspicion. He *had* been in love with SherryAnne.

"She was a beautiful woman," Jolyn observed. "And sexy." When SherryAnne turned on the charm, few men could resist her.

"She told me she and Chase were separated and planning a divorce. I swear, Jolyn, I wouldn't have slept with her under any other circumstances."

"She deceived you."

He shook his head. Sighed. "She and Chase had hit one

hell of a rough patch. He was interning with a veterinarian part-time and going to school full-time. SherryAnne didn't like being left alone at night, liked her job at the Clip and Curl even less. I'm pretty sure they would have divorced if she hadn't wound up pregnant. She stayed with Chase because he's Mandy's father." Steven turned an unwavering gaze on Jolyn. "I'm not just trying to shirk my responsibilities."

Steven made a valid argument. And his conviction wasn't easy to dismiss.

"I was only with SherryAnne that one time after she and Chase were married and only because she sought me out. Not the other way around."

"I believe you."

"But it wasn't our first time together."

Stunned, Jolyn gaped at her brother. "You're not joking."

"I wish I were." His shoulders slumped a little more with each confession he made. "Every time she and Chase were on the outs, SherryAnne came running to me. It started the year I was sixteen."

"Sixteen!" Jolyn was flabbergasted. "We would have been fourteen then." Chase and SherryAnne's romance was in the beginning stages those days. Puppy love more than anything else.

"We didn't sleep together until the night of your senior dance. Remember, I came home that weekend to help Dad paint the house?"

The same night Chase had kissed Jolyn on her parents' front porch. She drew in a sharp breath, feeling like someone had sucker punched her in the stomach. Chase and Sherry-Anne had been having one of their fights and had left the dance early. Later that night, he'd shown up at Jolyn's house and they'd kissed. SherryAnne had gone to Steven and… and… Oh, God! Jolyn fought a wave of nausea.

The day after the dance, Chase and SherryAnne had reconciled. Hurt and disappointed, Jolyn had given up on Chase and her girlhood crush once and for all. Steven, apparently, was another story. She didn't know how often SherryAnne had gone running to him and didn't want to know. Her heart couldn't take it.

She'd realized long ago that SherryAnne was less than perfect but this went beyond anything she'd ever imagined. How could she have been so blind?

"I'm not proud of what I did." Steven flung the last bit of his second hot dog to the waiting birds, who instantly dove on it. "SherryAnne took advantage of me to get back at Chase. But it's not like I said no to her even after I got wise to her games. She kept both Chase and me on her own personal leash for years."

Jolyn considered telling Steven he wasn't a trained dog and could have gotten away from SherryAnne, then realized he had. Only it might have been too late.

"In a way, she still has us both on leashes."

"How so?" Was her brother still pining for SherryAnne?

"By not admitting which one of us is Mandy's real father."

"Has she ever threatened you?"

"Not seriously." Steven picked up his soda and polished off the last of it. "She hinted at coming after me for child support, but I'm pretty sure she was just blowing smoke."

"Because she can't prove you're Mandy's father?"

"Right."

"Have you told Mom this?"

"Not all of it. Not the part about SherryAnne coming around since high school. She thinks I only slept with her that once."

"Maybe if you did tell Mom, she'd leave Chase alone."

Steven's eyebrows came together in a pronounced V.

"A lot of good could possibly come of it."

He shot her a chagrined look. "Here I am, thirty-one years old, and still scared to tell my mom I screwed up."

"You were young, and it was a long time ago. She'll get

over it." Jolyn smiled, her spirits lifting. All these years her mother had been clinging to a false hope because she didn't know the whole story.

At the sound of squealing tires, both her and Steven's heads jerked up. Their parents' white SUV barreled into the parking lot and came to a brake-grinding stop in front of Jolyn's office. She and her brother were on their feet before their father fully emerged from the driver's side.

"Dad! Hey, Dad."

He hurried toward them. "Steven! What are you doing here?"

"I told Mom yesterday I was coming."

"You di— Never mind. I'm glad to see you no matter the reason." He clapped his son on the back only to pull his hand back and rake his fingers through his hair.

"What's wrong, Dad?" Jolyn asked with rising concern. "I thought you and Mom were on your way to Pineville."

"Pineville?" Steven asked. "Why didn't you tell me?"

Their father's gaze went straight to Jolyn. "Your mother's refusing to go to the doctor. She canceled her appointment and won't make another one."

Chapter Nine

Turning the key to his post office box, Chase withdrew a stack of mail. Included among the bills, catalogs and sale flyers was a pink, laminated ticket. Milt Sutherland used the tickets to let customers know they had a package ready for pickup.

Chase's face was a familiar one at the front counter. With the nearest warehouse three hours away in Phoenix, most of his veterinary supplies and medicines were shipped to him. Since starting construction at his house, pink tickets appeared in his post office box on an almost daily basis as items for the new clinic arrived.

Chase rang the bell and waited for Milt to appear from the back. The town of Blue Ridge didn't provide door-to-door mail service. If residents wished to receive mail, they rented a post office box. Up until eight years ago, homes hadn't had formal street numbers. After much pressure from delivery services such as FedEx and UPS, the town had assigned addresses. Only people outside of Blue Ridge used them.

To Chase's surprise, Kenny Jr. came through the door separating the back from the front. A teddy bear of a man, Kenny Jr. did a little of everything around town, from working part-time at the Raintree ranch to being a member of the volunteer fire department.

"Hey, Chase. What's up?"

"Nothing much. On my way to the Holleran place. Where's Milt today?"

"Funny you should ask," Kenny Jr. said, taking Chase's ticket from his outstretched hand. "When he called and asked me to cover for him, he said he and Dottie were going to Pineville for the afternoon."

"And they're not?"

"Mrs. Cutter came by not ten minutes ago to pick up a shipment. She said Milt tore into the market parking lot like he was a driver in the Indianapolis 500. Next thing, him and Jolyn and Steven all left at the same time, one after the other in a big ol' caravan."

"Steven was there?"

"Guess so. Mrs. Cutter said something must be going on with them. Something bad. Milt's been acting kinda funny-like and so has Jolyn."

Chase agreed, at least where Jolyn was concerned. And he was becoming increasingly worried about her.

"Heard you guys found that boy yesterday." Kenny Jr. let out a long whistle. "Weren't he a lucky son of a gun?"

"Yeah." Chase was suddenly in a hurry. "How about that package?"

"Sure thing." Kenny Jr. ambled to the back room.

One minute stretched into two, then three. Tapping his truck keys on the counter, Chase wondered what in the world was going on with Jolyn's family. Steven's visit was nothing out of the ordinary but the same couldn't be said for Milt taking off work. Add to that a speed-racing display and mass exit home and the evidence mounted.

"You mind giving me a hand?" Kenny Jr. called. "This is more'n I can carry."

The package turned out to be three large, flat boxes containing the unassembled holding kennels Chase ordered for the new clinic. The boxes were more unwieldy than heavy. He and Kenny Jr. loaded them into the back of Chase's truck, securing them with bungee cords. Once he got home, Mike or one of the laborers could help him unload.

Waving goodbye to Kenny Jr., Chase pulled out of the parking lot. The Hollerans lived west, about a mile and a half. Jolyn also lived west, about a half mile. Hardly out of his way.

Chase decided to drive by Jolyn's parents' house. What he saw when he cruised past did nothing to assure him his concern was misplaced.

All four of the Sutherlands were standing in the open garage, having what was obviously a heated discussion. If they noticed Chase, they gave no indication. He traveled about 150 feet farther before pulling to a stop along the side of the road.

He wouldn't go back, wouldn't intrude on Jolyn and her family. He had no right. But Dottie's insistence on DNA testing and Steven's presence convinced him that whatever was causing such strife in the Sutherland family probably had something to do with him and Mandy.

Chase slammed the heel of his hand on the steering wheel. It looked like he'd been right about Dottie all along. She'd stopped pressuring him of late only because she was gathering her forces.

Was she trying to use Jolyn to get to him? And had Steven, after all these years of staying away, decided to join his mother's campaign?

Chase started his truck and hit the gas. The rear tires skidded and swerved before gaining traction, sending a shower of dirt and pebbles into the air.

He was crazy to think he could have a relationship with Jolyn, friendship or otherwise. Keeping Mandy safe and by his side mattered the most. Starting today—*this minute*—he'd steer clear of Jolyn and the oh so risky temptations she presented.

* * *

"You *have to call* your doctor and make a new appointment."

Jolyn followed her mother around the garage, determined to talk some sense into her. Her father and brother leaned against the workbench, watching in stoic silence. They'd already taken their turns with Dottie, who'd listened but remained unaffected.

Steven's admission about his long-standing affair with SherryAnne clearly unnerved Dottie but had no effect on her decision to cancel her doctor's appointment.

Ignoring Jolyn for the most part, she sorted through various boxes and bins and trunks stored along one wall of the garage.

"Mom," Jolyn pleaded. "This is serious. If it weren't, your doctor wouldn't have insisted on seeing you right away."

"I know that."

"Great. Then I'll just bring you the phone and you can call for a new appointment."

"Not today."

Jolyn bit back an angry retort. Her mother's refusal to listen to reason was getting old fast.

"I told you, I'll call next week." Dottie bent to lift a crate full of old tap shoes and ballet slippers wrapped in plastic and sorted by size.

Jolyn's father beat her to the punch, attempting to take the crate away from her before she got a firm hold of it. "You shouldn't be overdoing it."

"I'm not an invalid, Milt."

"Dottie." He scowled at her until she relinquished the crate. "Where do you want it?"

"Over there." She pointed to a shelf. "Careful of the make-up cases."

"Jolyn's right." Steven pulled a three-legged stool out from beneath the workbench and set it near his mother, then gestured for her to sit down.

"What's with you and your father?" Dottie asked, frowning.

"They're worried about you." Jolyn guided her mother toward the stool. "Me, too. You haven't been sleeping well for weeks." And she wasn't eating well. Clothes had started to hang on her already trim dancer's figure.

"You probably need a rest more than me." Dottie stared fixedly at Jolyn's knee.

"I'm doing better. Mostly because I've been following my doctor's orders. Unlike someone else."

Her mother grumbled. "If I sit for a few minutes, will you—all of you—quit pestering me?"

"We will about taking it easy. Not about rescheduling your appointment."

"Fine." Dottie plopped down onto the stool and hooked one heel on the bottom rung. Her mother usually didn't give up so readily. She must really be sick or scared or both.

"I wish you'd quit ganging up on me." Dottie squirmed under her family's scrutiny. Without intending to, Jolyn, Steven and their father had formed a circle around her. No wonder she felt like the subject of an intervention.

"We love you, Mom," Steven said. "And we don't like that you're ignoring what could be a serious health condition." He'd taken the news of his mother's medical problems as expected. He felt anger that he wasn't informed sooner, concerned for her health, and, like the rest of them, frustrated at her perpetual stalling.

Dottie compressed her lips into a thin line. She didn't, however, cry as Jolyn thought she might. Instead, she hopped off the stool and pushed between Jolyn and her brother. "I have a lot to do."

"What's so important?" Jolyn struggled to maintain her cool.

"Final costume fittings are tonight at six-thirty."

"For what?" Steven asked. The three of them stared at Dottie's back while she rummaged through boxes.

"Red, White and Blue Ridge Days," Jolyn answered.

Every year on the weekend before the Fourth of July, the town put on a two-day celebration that included a horse show and gymkhana, craft fair, bingo tournament and a barbecue chicken dinner in the community center, followed by a dance. Before the band took the stage, Dottie's advanced students performed a selection of their best numbers. It was one of the highlights of the celebration and something the students and Dottie worked on for months beforehand.

"Is that why you canceled your appointment, Mom?" Jolyn asked. "Because of the performance this Saturday?" It wouldn't surprise her if her mother had put her students' needs ahead of her own.

Dottie shook her head.

"You sure?"

She nodded, her shoulders shaking slightly.

Jolyn suddenly realized her mother *was* crying. "Mom? Are you okay?"

Dottie sniffed.

Jolyn's father rushed forward to envelop his wife in a hug. "Sweetheart?"

She broke into tears, blurting, "I'm sorry. So sorry."

"For what?" He tenderly stroked her hair.

"I didn't cancel my appointment." She buried her face in her husband's shirt. "My doctor did."

"Why?"

Fear swept through Jolyn. She reached for Steven's hand. He returned her urgent grip.

"The lumps appear suspicious," her mother said between tiny sobs. "Rather than waste any time, he wants to admit me to Pineville General right away and perform a biopsy."

Chapter Ten

"'Bye, honey. You be good for Mrs. Payne, okay?" Chase accepted a sticky kiss from his daughter, who went right back to picking at her pancakes.

"I will. I love you, Daddy."

A little more enthusiasm would be nice but unlikely given SherryAnne's phone call the previous night.

"Love you, too." He tugged on Mandy's earlobe until she finally cracked a smile, unable to take his eyes off her. What had he ever done to deserve such a rare and beautiful treasure? He vowed to do anything, take on an entire army of Sherry-Annes and Dotties if need be, rather than lose her.

"What's wrong?" Mandy asked. "You look funny."

Chase snatched a napkin from the holder and wiped her chin. "You're the one who looks funny." That earned him a giggle, albeit a small one. He'd take what he could get. "Gotta go. Be good for Mrs. Payne."

He went out the kitchen door and, since Anita had yet to arrive, walked around the side of the house to the clinic. Jolyn and her crew had been making excellent progress, and he should tell her so.

Chase immediately suffered a twinge of regret. He'd been avoiding Jolyn as much as possible since Monday when he'd driven by her parents' house, and it was now Friday. Four whole days. He was, admittedly, miserable but still convinced he'd made the right decision. Though Dottie had yet to show her hand, he wasn't taking any chances where Mandy was concerned.

SherryAnne's call last night had sent his daughter into an emotional tailspin. Apologizing again for postponing her visit—she had some rodeo to attend—SherryAnne promised a big surprise for Mandy that would arrive on her birthday. Rather than making Mandy feel better, the announcement had the opposite effect.

There were times when Chase wished his ex-wife would drop off the edge of the earth. Then, he'd come to his senses and remember Mandy needed even the small amount of attention her mother paid her.

At the clinic entrance he stopped briefly to smile again over the hand and paw prints in the concrete step. Pushing open the door, he stepped inside and was immediately accosted by an overpowering smell. Noting the newly painted walls and recently installed ceiling lights in his reception area, he followed the sound of voices and clatter to his examining room.

A trio of workers, two men and one woman, were applying a fresh coat of paint to the bare walls using long-handled rollers. Blue masking tape covered the doorjamb and windowpanes, protecting them from accidental splatter. Wires protruded from square holes in the walls that light switch, electrical outlet and phone jack plates would eventually cover. Flooring and cabinets had not yet been installed and wouldn't be until the first of the week. The timing was a bit tricky as the bulk of Chase's equipment was due to arrive a week from today and construction had to be done before then.

"Morning, Doc," one of the painters greeted Chase. "How's it looking?"

"Nice." Chase nodded approvingly. "I like it."

Jolyn had been right about the color. The pale green not only made the room look bigger and brighter, but the soft hue also had a soothing quality his patients' owners would appreciate.

"We'll finish the walls today," the painter informed Chase. "And be back in the morning for the trim."

"You're working on Saturday?"

"Yeah. Jolyn found a place for us to stay the night and told us if we finished by noon, we could bum around town the rest of the weekend. Been told you folks got quite a deal going on here." He dipped the roller in a pan of paint and carefully scraped off the excess.

"We do. Red, White and Blue Ridge Days." Chase would be at the community center most of Saturday morning. He'd entered Matilda in several of the horse show classes and planned to stick around for any veterinarian emergencies. Mandy would be there, too. She couldn't wait for the dance performance later that evening. "Where you staying?" Chase had heard the local inn was booked to capacity.

"Cots and sleeping bags in Jolyn's garage but we don't mind, do we?" the painter asked his coworkers. "Long as we get to stay."

"Are there going to be any fireworks?" the woman asked. Shorter than average and built like a fire hydrant, she handled the roller with uncommon confidence and grace.

"No, it's too dry this summer. The Forest Service won't permit it."

Chase's cousin, Gage, and the rest of the volunteer fire department would be at the celebration just in case any youngsters got the bright idea to put on their own fireworks display. Mike Flannigan had done just that when they were kids, burning about a quarter acre of pasture out behind the community center before the volunteer fire department finally extinguished the blaze. The irony that Mike was now a firefighter himself wasn't lost on him or anyone in town.

"Your office is done if you want to have a look at that," the first painter said. "Came out real nice."

Chase checked his watch and saw that he had a few minutes before Anita arrived. "Think I will. Thanks."

They were heading back to the Double S Ranch for another round of semen collection. His new assistant hadn't exaggerated her charms. She'd handled the owner's Brahma bull, Peaches, like he was a toy poodle and not the size of a small elephant. Ranchers in the vicinity, whose initial reaction to the diminutive female was to scoff, were being won over, though not as fast as Peaches. Last weekend Anita had moved into a rented room until she could locate something more permanent, becoming Blue Ridge's newest resident.

Chase's plan was coming together like clockwork. The clinic was almost complete and should be open for business within the next two weeks. His new assistant displayed great promise. And, most importantly, he'd spent more time with Mandy recently than he had in the last two years.

He should be ecstatic. Delighted, at the very least. Instead, his feet dragged as he went down the tiny hall to his office.

Jolyn.

Somehow, without him really noticing, she'd gotten under his skin. Problem was, he liked having her there.

Give it time, Chase told himself. *Sooner or later you'll forget about her.*

Yeah, like in another fifty or sixty years.

Careful not to touch the walls with their wet paint, he entered his office—and drew up short at the unexpected sight of Jolyn sitting on the floor, unpacking fluorescent lightbulbs from a cardboard carton.

"Oh, sorry," he mumbled, then realizing how stupid he sounded, said, "How's it going?"

"Hey, Chase." She spared him a quick glance before returning to her task, but it was long enough for him to spot the hurt in her eyes.

He bit back a curse, berating himself for being such a jerk. She had no idea why he'd suddenly distanced himself from her, knew only that he'd pulled a Houdini for no apparent reason just when they were growing closer.

Dammit! Could he have screwed up any worse? Jolyn had always supported him when it came to Mandy. He'd been wrong not to explain his recent behavior.

Maybe it wasn't too late.

"I didn't realize you were here." The instant the words were out of his mouth he wanted to retract them. Jolyn's ramrod-straight spine told him she'd misconstrued his remark and probably thought he was unhappy at finding her there. "I didn't see your truck outside," he said, trying to amend his blunder.

"Mike took it over to Ace's Auto this morning," she said tightly. "The alternator's been acting up."

"Need any help with that?" When she didn't tell him to take a hike, Chase inched closer.

"I can manage, thanks." She crawled to her feet and, with a bulb in one hand, positioned the aluminum stepladder directly beneath the ceiling light.

Chase got his first good look at her in days and was shocked at her appearance. "Jeez, Jolyn. Are you all right?"

Dark circles shadowed her eyes, lines of fatigue bracketed her mouth and she moved as if every joint in her body ached.

Chase was suddenly furious with himself. How could he have been so insensitive and hurt her like he obviously had? She couldn't control her mother any more than he could his.

"I'm okay," she said and climbed the first step of the ladder.

"Jolyn."

She stopped in place and with her back to him, said, "Look, I'm sorry for being so scarce this past week."

"What?" *She'd* been scarce?

"I've had a lot going on and don't want you to think I was avoiding you."

"How did your CAT scan go?" he asked, wondering if her knee was responsible for her weary appearance. Jolyn hadn't mentioned the procedure to him, but she had to Mrs. Cutter, so most of Blue Ridge probably knew by now.

"Good. Everything's normal." She continued up the ladder and inserted the bulb into the light fixture. With a flicker and a series of tiny pings, the bulb came on, filling the room with light.

Before she could climb back down, Chase said, "Wait," and handed her another bulb from the carton. She might have refused his help but was going to get it nonetheless.

Hesitantly, she took the bulb.

He bit back another curse. Talk around town was that the Sutherlands were having some kind of big trouble, though no one knew the exact nature of it. Chase made an educated guess. Since Jolyn's knee was fine and business was going well—he'd learned from Mike that she'd landed a job building a solarium—it must be about him and Mandy. Were the Sutherlands divided over Dottie's attempt to prove Steven was Mandy's biological father?

It seemed that Chase and Jolyn had avoided each other all week for the same reason—her mother. Damn Dottie and her meddling. She had to know how much grief and misery she was causing people, including those she loved. Chase's resolve to steer clear of Jolyn weakened. When the second lightbulb flickered to life, he reached down for another one.

"Are you going to Red, White and Blue Ridge Days this weekend?" Casual conversation, he decided, might help.

"Not in the morning. I have too much going on. I'm planning on dropping by in the afternoon and maybe on Sunday."

"What about the dinner tomorrow night?"

Chase picked up the last bulb. As he stood, Jolyn shifted and he found himself staring at her curvaceous backside.

His hormones evidently hadn't listened to all those talks he gave himself about cooling it with Jolyn, because his libido behaved like one of those fluorescent bulbs she'd just inserted, flickering to life in an instant. When she raised her arm to wipe away a smudge of dust, he followed the long, luscious line of her body. Dangerous ground on which to tread, but Chase was powerless to resist.

"Can't miss that," she said.

"Huh?" He shook his head to clear it. "Oh, yeah, the dinner."

"Could you pass me the cover while you're at it?"

Chase responded automatically, handing her the pliable plastic rectangle. He was rewarded with another great view of Jolyn stretching.

When she finished snapping the cover in place, he retreated several steps, giving her room to climb down the ladder. He should have closed his eyes or, better yet, left the room. Watching her hips move back and forth at such close range was pure torture. Reaching the floor, she spun to face him. Chase wasted no time closing the distance between them.

"Oh! Excuse me."

That was his cue to move away, only he didn't take it. He'd missed her these last four days, wanted her more than he could remember wanting a woman. And if sharing the same tiny space for a few brief moments was all he'd ever have of her, fine. He'd settle for what he could get.

"What about the dance after the dinner? You going?" His hands itched to hold her almost as much as his mouth craved the taste of hers.

"Yes." She stared up at him with liquid hazel eyes that destroyed the last vestiges of his willpower. "Of course." It was on the tip of Chase's tongue to ask her to save him a dance when she said, "Mom's advanced students are performing. I can't miss that."

Her mother. At the mention of Dottie, Chase's ardor waned.

Just as well. Anita had arrived.

"Chase? Where are you?"

"In here," he answered flatly and did what he should have done five minutes ago—put a respectable distance between him and Jolyn.

Wordlessly, she moved the ladder and positioned it under the second light fixture. By the time Anita joined them in the office, she'd climbed up the ladder, and Chase was holding a bulb out to her.

"This is great!" Anita gushed, her wandering gaze taking in every detail. "It's really coming along."

"Thanks," Chase said. "But my contractor deserves all the credit."

"Hi, Anita," Jolyn said over her shoulder.

They'd met briefly on two occasions when Anita had come by the house to go on a call with Chase.

"Hey, Jolyn. How's it going?"

"Not bad for a Friday."

While friendly, Jolyn's banter lacked its usual warmth, and she made a point of not looking at Chase. He wondered if his abrupt brush-off was to blame.

"Will I see you at the horse show tomorrow?" Head tilted back, Anita watched Jolyn.

"No, I've got work in the morning."

As they'd done with the first light, Chase passed Jolyn bulbs and she installed them.

"You aren't entering that horse of yours in the gymkhana?" Anita asked. "I've heard the two of you can clear some pretty spectacular jumps."

"I don't jump anymore," Jolyn replied, an edge to her voice. "Not since the accident."

"Oh, um, yeah." Anita winced at Chase, clearly mortified at her unintentional slip. Trying to recover, she said, "Sorry if brought up something I shouldn't have."

"Don't sweat it." Jolyn inserted the last bulb.

"We should head out," Chase told Anita. "Peaches is expecting you." The time for a quick exit was long overdue.

Chase would have liked to help Jolyn with the ladder but she had it collapsed and on the floor before he had the chance. She did it all without looking at him or Anita.

Great. So much for alleviating the tension of the last week. With a casual "See you later," he motioned for Anita to accompany him outside.

"Sorry if I blew it in there," she said when they were seated in Chase's truck.

"You didn't. Don't worry about it."

"Sure?"

"Yeah, I am." If anyone had blown it in there, it was him.

JOLYN WATCHED Chase and Anita drive away, all the while fighting a wretched case of jealousy. Not at Anita, but at the easy camaraderie she shared with Chase. The same camaraderie Jolyn had once shared with him but had lost this past week.

For a few seconds, when they were standing so close she could feel his breath caress her cheek and sense his potent sexual response to her nearness, she'd almost let it slip about the lumps in her mother's breast. Then, he'd have known that her reasons for avoiding him lately had nothing to do with them.

But then Anita had shown up. Chase had left with her, and Jolyn was back to where she'd been before he'd found her installing the lights in his office—alone and miserable.

Speaking of lights…

Jolyn hefted the ladder and walked tiredly to the surgery. She'd like to blame work or her knee for her lack of energy, but she knew stress was the real culprit.

The Sutherlands had fallen into a routine. Jolyn's mother pretended nothing was wrong and refused to talk about the lumps, the biopsy, or *anything* until after Red, White and Blue Ridge Days. Jolyn, her father and her brother, however, did talk, often and at great length, trying to figure out how they could convince Dottie to get the help she needed.

The constant tension was having an adverse effect on everyone in the family. Her father in particular, whose temper flared at the least little provocation.

The one and only good thing to come out of this terrible mess was that her mother hadn't mentioned Chase or Mandy in four whole days. Whether that minor miracle had to do with what Steven had told her about him and SherryAnne, the advanced class dance performance tomorrow night, or the unsettling news her doctor had imparted in his phone call, Jolyn didn't know.

Something told her, however, that her mother hadn't given up, simply taken a break.

Jolyn knew she was crazy to think she and Chase could ever be together. But she couldn't stop hoping....

"Hi, Jolyn. Whatcha doing?"

Buzz and Lickety popped around the corner seconds ahead of Mandy.

"Installing lightbulbs. What about you?"

"Nothing." She dragged the word out. "Waiting for Mrs. Payne. She's doing some stuff in the house."

By "stuff," Jolyn assumed Mandy meant household chores. "You can help me if you want."

Mandy shrugged indifferently. "Could, I suppose."

Lickety dropped to the floor and rolled onto her back, silently begging for a tummy scratching. Mandy paid her no attention, which was unheard of. She always had a pet for the pitifully homely but endearingly affectionate dog. The little girl must really be down in the dumps today.

Well, that made two of them.

"Have you ever painted a room?"

A tiny spark of interest flittered across Mandy's face. "No."

"Want to try?"

"You'd let me?"

"Sure." Jolyn smiled for the first time that day. Maybe she couldn't smooth out things between her and Chase but she could lift his daughter's spirits. She picked up the ladder and said, "Bring that carton of bulbs, will you?"

Mandy needed three attempts before she got a solid grip. "Where to?"

"The reception area. Follow me."

Ten minutes later, with the painters' help, Mandy was busy slathering paint onto the storage room walls, getting as much or more on the floor and the oversized T-shirt Jolyn had borrowed for her to wear. She told the painters to let the girl have her fun and then repaint the walls later.

Installing the last of the florescent lightbulbs, she went to check on Mandy's progress and was gratified to see the girl grinning from ear to ear. Buzz and Lickety were a different story and lay sulking in a corner. Judging by the pale green dog prints dotting the floor, one or both of them had gotten into the pan of paint.

"How's it coming?" Jolyn asked.

"I'm almost done."

"Good, because Mrs. Payne said to let you know you'll be leaving in about fifteen minutes."

That might be cutting it close, Jolyn thought. It would take ten minutes alone just to get the paint out of Mandy's hair and off her face and hands.

"My mom called last night," Mandy said without preamble and without taking her eyes off the wall.

"She did?" Given Mandy's previously forlorn mood, Jolyn felt fairly confident SherryAnne hadn't changed her mind about coming out for a visit.

"She told me she has a surprise for me and that it'll be here for my birthday."

"That's nice." Jolyn tried to sound enthused. "I bet you can't wait."

A long silence followed, the soft *clack, clack* of the roller hitting the wall the only sound.

"Do you have any idea what it is?" Jolyn's second attempt to generate conversation also failed. She sympathized with the little girl, who was so obviously miserable.

Before she could come up with something else to say, Mandy spat out, "I'm glad she's not coming to see me. I hope she never comes here again."

"Oh, sweetie, you don't mean that."

"I do. I hate her." Mandy threw down the roller. Startled, the dogs scrambled to their feet and bolted from the room, crashing into the wall and getting paint on their fur. "You can be my dad's girlfriend if you want because I don't care anymore." She stormed out of the room behind the dogs, ripping off her T-shirt and tossing it onto the floor.

Jolyn stooped to pick up the discarded roller and carried it over to the pan of paint. The floor was a disaster area. Large splatters covered most of the dog prints. It didn't matter, she reflected. Once the flooring was installed, no one would ever see the mess underneath.

She wished every problem in her life could be resolved so easily.

Chapter Eleven

Seven gypsy princesses, their full skirts swishing and gold bracelets clinking, dashed past Jolyn. Not one of them was over the age of fifteen.

"Nice job, ladies," she called, patting the shoulders within reach.

The audience agreed, continuing to applaud. A few of the more enthusiastic fans yelled, "Encore, encore!"

Dottie's advanced students had put on yet another outstanding performance for Red, White and Blue Ridge Days.

Jolyn walked around behind the stage and into absolute chaos. "Do you need any help, Mom?" she asked. The hallway off the community center's huge kitchen had been converted into a temporary dressing room. Seven girls and three costume changes, coupled with cramped quarters and two helpers, equaled a disaster area.

"Thanks, honey, but we're in good shape." Dottie appeared to be unaffected by all the commotion. She glided through the room, restoring order and calm wherever she went.

"I can take those boxes to the car for you."

"Your dad will. You know him, he has a system." Her mother was the one with the system, her father merely carried it out.

"Okay." Jolyn lingered, unable to explain her urge to stay amid the dancers when she more often couldn't wait to flee.

"Go on." Dottie shooed Jolyn away. "The band will be starting any minute. Have some fun why don't you? You deserve it."

She didn't feel much in the mood for fun and hadn't all week.

"I'll be fine." Her mother smiled and cupped her cheek, the gesture reminiscent of when Jolyn was the same age as the girls. "Really. *Everything* will be fine. You'll see."

Her mother understood what Jolyn hadn't and had offered exactly the reassurance she needed.

"I know." Jolyn gave her mother a brief, yet fierce, hug.

"I'll be out shortly." Dottie turned her attention to a student. "Your father's promised to two-step with me."

Jolyn always liked watching her parents dance, be it country-western, like tonight, ballroom, disco, or whatever. Over the course of many years, and with her mother's patient tutoring, her father had progressed into a passably good dance partner.

The band was on the stage and warming up when Jolyn returned to the main room. Folding tables and chairs had been moved to create an open area in front of the stage. Fruit punch and iced tea dispensers were set up on a table in the back. A pair of doors on the side of the building were open, allowing people to travel back and forth to the picnic area for a breath of fresh air. Jolyn and Chase had sat at one of those very picnic tables the afternoon she'd presented her bid for his clinic.

Hard to believe nearly a month had gone by since then.

Jolyn found a group of her parents' neighbors and, at their warm insistence, joined them. She hadn't had much free time for socializing since her return home and tried to enjoy herself. Relaxing was difficult, and she listened more than she contributed to the conversation. Scanning the ever-moving crowd, her restless gaze came to a halt only when she found Chase.

She'd spotted him earlier in the dinner line, watched him

and Mandy eat from the corner of her eye, and knew where they were sitting during the dance performance. With almost two hundred people packed into a room designed to accommodate a hundred and fifty, it was easy to keep out of his path.

Was that what she wanted?

No. She'd much prefer going back to the way things had been before Monday when her mother had told them about her doctor's phone call. Unfortunately, that didn't appear to be possible.

Mike came in from outside and stopped to chat with Jolyn and her friends. The topic quickly turned to the clinic with everyone wanting to know how it was coming along. Fortunately, Mike answered most of the questions, leaving Jolyn free to brood some more.

The band launched into their first set, opening it with a rousing country classic. Rather than be quiet and listen, everyone just talked louder. By the start of the third number, Jolyn was ready to go home, but knew her absence would be noticed and gossiped about.

She had just decided to excuse herself when Mike touched her arm and said, "Would you like to dance?"

"Um…" Jolyn laughed nervously. She hadn't been on the dance floor in she didn't remember how long. Touring, with its sixteen-hour workdays, didn't allow for an active night life. And for six months after the accident, Jolyn hadn't known if she would walk again, much less dance.

"Come on," Mike said, reaching for her hand. "When was the last time you and I tripped the light fantastic?"

Eleven years. Their high-school senior dance. The same night Chase had kissed Jolyn and SherryAnne had sought out Steven for a whole lot more than kissing.

Before she could decline Mike's invitation, he whisked her out onto the floor. The song had one of those in-between tempos, not too fast, not too slow. Jolyn had trouble keeping up with him, though not because of her knee. She was out of practice, and he was an energetic dancer.

"Take it easy," she said, slightly out of breath.

"Sorry." He grinned apologetically and in his best Bullwinkle the Moose imitation, said, "Sometimes I don't know my own strength."

"It's me. I'm not in the best of shape anymore."

The blatant up and down he gave her was pure male. "News flash, Jolyn. You're in great shape." As if to emphasize his point, he tugged her closer.

She instinctively hung on. It was that or fall flat on her face. She liked Mike, enjoyed working with him. However, she wasn't interested in him romantically. She hoped he wasn't thinking of rekindling their high-school courtship. It had been one-sided back then and would be again today.

"I want to thank you for giving me a job," he said, smiling down at her. "I know it may not be permanent and all, but I really appreciate it."

"You're doing great. It's me who appreciates you."

"Can't say I ever thought I'd have a woman for a boss."

"You getting a lot of flack from your buddies?"

"Hell, yes. I tell them they're just jealous. None of that fat bunch of slobs has ever worked for a boss as pretty as mine." He anchored his arm more firmly around her waist and spun her in a half circle.

"You're making me dizzy." She chastised him with light-hearted humor. Inside, she was growing increasingly agitated. Mike was flirting with her and she wasn't sure how to take it.

Finally, the song ended. "Thanks, Mike. I enjoyed that more than I thought I would."

Before she could break away, he said, "Wait." The next number started, and he swept her into his arms for another dance. "There's something I want to ask you."

Oh, boy. Here it comes. Jolyn searched her mind for a kind letdown.

Mike lowered his head. His lips hovered a few inches from her ear. "The thing is—"

Jolyn couldn't hear herself think over the loud music and the people talking.

"—I don't know how to say it so I guess I'll just come out with it—"

She'd tell him, *I like you too much as an employee and a friend to risk ruining things by entering into a personal relationship.* Yes, that's how she'd handle it.

"Oh, hell." Mike chuckled sheepishly. "I'm acting like a dumb kid. Here it goes." He inhaled robustly.

Jolyn braced herself. Mike was a super guy. She'd hate having to hurt his feelings.

"Do you think Anita would go out with me if I asked her?"

"What?" Jolyn came to a sudden standstill in the middle of the dance floor. "Anita!" She could have burst out laughing with relief but didn't in case Mike took it the wrong way.

"She'll turn me down flat, won't she?" He was wearing one of those kicked-puppy faces Mrs. Cutter had been talking about the other day.

"No, no. It's not that." Jolyn didn't dare tell him what had been running through her mind before he'd mentioned Anita's name. "I've only met her once or twice. I hardly know her."

"She probably has a boyfriend." After the third couple bumped into them, Mike and Jolyn resumed dancing. "Girls like her have guys lining up at their doorstep."

"She is pretty."

"Has Chase mentioned anything to you?"

Jolyn shook her head. "He hasn't." Mike's inadvertent reminder of Jolyn and Chase's awkward meeting the previous morning took a little of the shine off her good mood. "But Anita recently rented a room in town. If she's involved with someone back in Phoenix, it can't be serious or she wouldn't have moved here."

Mike's face lit up. "You're right. Thanks." Taking Jolyn by complete surprise, he leaned down and kissed her soundly, though chastely, on the lips. "She's here somewhere. You won't mind if I abandon you and go looking for her?"

"Not at all." Jolyn felt her cheeks warm. "Good luck."

Humming along with the band, Mike twirled Jolyn, caught her up in his arms and then proceeded to Cotton-Eye Joe her across the floor.

"Take it easy," Jolyn complained good-naturedly. She was once more having trouble keeping up with him.

Mike pulled her up short. It took Jolyn a few disorienting seconds to realize it was because they'd nearly collided with someone—someone who stood like a stone statue in their path.

"Hey, pal!" Mike said amiably. "Didn't see you there."

His smile wasn't returned.

Holding out a hand to Jolyn, Chase said, "Mind if I cut in?"

JOLYN DIDN'T COME willingly into Chase's arms. She might not have come at all if Mike hadn't nudged her along. For someone who'd been practically mauling her in public, he appeared unconcerned by another man absconding with his dance partner.

Was that because Mike didn't consider Chase competition? Settling a hand on the small of Jolyn's back, Chase decided to give her superintendent a serious run for his money.

Luck was on his side. No sooner did he and Jolyn take to the floor than the band switched to a different number, one with a slower, sultry tempo.

With Jolyn pressed so close their hips bumped with each step, and it was hard for Chase not to imagine taking her to bed. Truth be told, he'd been thinking of little else lately.

Watching her dance with Mike, standing idly by while the other man's hands roamed all over her, had made Chase crazy with jealousy. He wanted it to be his arms circling her waist, his shoulder she rested her head on, his lips kissing hers. He would have remained in the dark corner where he'd taken refuge all night if Mike hadn't laid one on Jolyn. Chase had barely refrained from wringing the son of a bitch's neck.

Rather than give the local sheriff a reason to arrest him, he'd asked to cut in.

He didn't regret his impulsiveness. Having Jolyn to himself, staring at the delectable V of bare skin showing through her open shirt collar, beat spending the night in jail by far.

"You're a much better dancer than you used to be," she said, raising her eyes to meet his.

The jolt from even that small contact went clear through Chase, and he missed a step. "Hannah's been teaching me." He didn't add that his cousin thought he should brush up on his skills in preparation for when he started dating again.

"I saw her earlier. And her friend. He seems nice."

"He's okay." Chase had no desire to talk about Hannah or her date or anyone else. He much preferred concentrating on Jolyn and her lush, lovely breasts, the tips of which rubbed across his shirtfront whenever she moved just so.

She apparently wasn't of the same opinion when it came to conversation.

"Your Aunt Susan and Uncle Joseph left a little while ago."

"Uncle Joseph's gout is acting up."

"Where's Mandy?"

"With Elizabeth."

"Did she enjoy the advanced students' performance?"

Chase turned his head so that their temples were touching and said in her ear, "Shut up, will you?" He slid his hand up her spine and then back down. Slowly, so that his fingers caressed each vertebra.

She let out a small gasp. It was the only sound she made for the rest of the dance.

He took full advantage of the silence. Fitting her more snugly in his embrace, he let go of her right hand in order to circle her waist with both arms. She had no choice but to link her arms around his neck. Swaying more than dancing, they moved to the music.

Chase realized it was time to stop kidding himself. His attraction to Jolyn had long passed the friendship stage.

So, what was he going to do about it?

He lifted a hand to her chin and tipped her head up, forcing her to look at him. God, she was amazingly beautiful and totally oblivious to it. In a flash, he made up his mind.

"Let's go."

"All right," she said, so softly he read her lips more than heard her speak.

Chase pulled Jolyn behind him, cutting a path through the dancing couples. If he didn't get her alone right then and there, the sheriff really would have a reason to arrest him.

Once outside, they passed the picnic area where old Mr. Parkerson sat chewing tobacco and sneaking sips from his flask of whiskey.

They didn't stop until they rounded the back corner of the building. Across the walkway was the competition arena where he'd won first place in two classes with Matilda that morning. He considered taking Jolyn under the bleachers, then vetoed that idea. Too many memories of him and SherryAnne as teenagers. Changing directions, he headed for the officials' booth, a small, block building to the right of the arena.

She didn't ask where they were going or what they were doing, not even when they ducked beneath the shelter of the overhanging roof.

Once they were hidden in the shadows, he trapped her between the side of the building and the equally unyielding length of his body, then forced himself to take it easy. Now

hat he had Jolyn to himself, there was no need to hurry.
Bracing his arms on either side of her head, he lowered his
mouth to claim hers.

The instant their tongues touched, someone set off a firecracker in the distance. Chase heard the whistle, felt the bang
as if it came from inside him. Another firecracker followed,
but by then he was so lost in Jolyn he barely noticed.

She returned each thrust of his tongue with one of her
own, exploring his mouth with the same eagerness he
explored hers. Unable to get enough, he moved his hands to
her waist. She moaned her pleasure into his mouth. He responded by brushing the undersides of her breasts with his
thumbs.

She didn't tell him to stop. If anything, she encouraged him
to take greater liberties by arching into him. He did so, covering
her breasts with his hands and shaping them to fit his palms.

Her breath hitched. His lodged in his throat. Another
minute of this and he would take her right there behind the
officials' booth.

A small voice in the back of his brain told him to stop. This
wasn't how he wanted his first time making love with Jolyn
to be—hiding in the dark with a third of the town not a
hundred feet away. He'd much rather woo Jolyn in a very
quiet, very secluded place. Dinner, candles, wine and lots of
moonlight. Then, when they finally came together, the resulting fireworks would put any Fourth of July celebration to
shame.

Another firecracker went off. A man hollered, "You kids
quit that before you set the field on fire." Youthful laughter
ensued and then the echo of running footsteps.

Reality returned and with it, reason.

Chase did the very last thing in the world he wanted to do
at that moment—he disengaged himself from Jolyn's embrace.

"We should get back to the dance." He was going to add

"Before anyone notices," but realized everyone probably had noticed their abrupt exit and there was nothing they could do to save themselves from the gossip mill.

He didn't care. Let people talk.

"Jolyn?"

"Yes," she murmured.

He took her hand, turned it over and raised it to his mouth. Unfurling her fingers, he pressed a kiss to the sensitive center of her palm, earning a wistful sigh for his efforts.

"I wouldn't have stopped if we weren't in such a public place," he said, continuing to hold her hand captive. After tonight, it would be difficult to get near her and not touch or hold her.

"That's the only reason I let you stop." Her hazel eyes, nearly black in the moonlight, sparkled with a mischief he hadn't seen since they were kids.

The awkwardness of the last week was gone, replaced with an intimacy shared by just the two of them. Chase dropped a quick kiss on her lips. They would make love, and soon, just not tonight. Folding her hand in his, they walked back to the community center and the dance.

"Sorry for breaking my promise," he said.

"What promise is that?"

"The one about not kissing you until the clinic was done."

"Close enough. We'll be finished next week."

"What are we going to do about us when that happens?" If Dottie heard about his and Jolyn's moonlight tryst, which she would unless she were blind, deaf and living in a cave, she might cause trouble for Jolyn. Chase was determined not to add to her difficulties.

"I'm not sure yet."

"If you're willing, I'd like to see where this thing with us goes."

She hesitated before answering, and Chase began to doubt

his spontaneous admission. But having had a taste of her passion, he wasn't sure he could give her up without a fight.

"There's this situation with my family. It's…complicated and not easily resolved."

"Does it involve me and Mandy?"

"Not directly. Though you might be affected."

"I don't understand." They approached the edge of the picnic area. As if by silent agreement, they stopped beside a light post.

"And I can't explain," she said. "Not yet. Maybe after Monday."

"What happens then?"

She shook her head. "I'd tell you if I could."

A personal matter that didn't directly involve him and Mandy? Chase's curiosity was piqued but he let the matter drop.

"Monday, huh?" His fingers glided up the length of her arm.

"Yeah."

"I suppose I can wait." Not that he had a choice. "Let me get you back inside to Mike."

"Mike?" She gave him an odd look.

"He's not your date tonight?"

"No. What gave you that idea?"

"The way he was coming on to you while you two were dancing."

She laughed. "He was asking me about Anita. It seems my superintendent has the hots for your assistant."

"I'll be damned." Chase's laughter joined hers. "Guess I have to take back all the rotten things I thought about him."

"What rotten things?"

"Never mind."

He took her by the elbow and escorted her inside. Instantly, two dozen pairs of eyes were fastened on them. Chase was able to ignore all the stares except one. He met Dottie's head-on without flinching.

Chapter Twelve

Jolyn sat at the dining room table, papers spread out all over the place, eraser shavings covering the tabletop and her lap. The small handheld calculator she'd been using since starting her business was giving her fits, and she promised herself she'd invest in a heavy-duty desktop model at the first opportunity.

"Does this exclude or include wallpaper?" her mother asked, studying the paper in front of her. "I can't read your handwriting." She was seated at a computer station tucked into one corner of the family room, typing a bid proposal for Jolyn. They could see each other and talk across the open arched doorway between the two rooms.

"Exclude," Jolyn answered, punching more numbers into the finicky calculator and calling it names under her breath.

Paperwork, in her opinion, was an evil necessity, and the ten hours a week she spent on it were the worst part of owning her own business.

If all went well, her new office would be ready to occupy in a few weeks. She wished it could be sooner, but paying work came first and then the repairs at Cutter's Market, most of which were done.

In the week since Red, White and Blue Ridge Days, she'd been asked to bid on a restroom renovation at Sage's Bar and

Grill and a storage shed at the school. Not quite the big jobs she needed to grow Sutherland Construction, but better than nothing. She reminded herself that most businesses operated at a loss their first year, a fact that didn't console her. Jolyn hoped to avoid being a statistic. To accomplish that, she'd have to win two or three jobs the size of Chase's clinic over the next six months.

Living in a small town worked both for and against her. Being the only licensed general contractor did give her an advantage. Unfortunately, a small population meant that there might not be enough work to keep her company afloat. If things didn't pick up, Jolyn would have to expand her territory to Pineville or Globe, where general contractors were plentiful and competition was stiff.

Paperwork wasn't the only downside, she thought dejectedly. If not for her parents, she wouldn't have made it this far, and she owed them a great deal.

Dottie had proven invaluable. She typed Jolyn's bids, placed phone calls for her, scheduled deliveries, checked on prices and balanced her books.

"You're going to need more than that laptop of yours when you move into your office," she said, lowering her reading glasses and peering at Jolyn over the rims.

"Yeah, I know." She cringed inside at the thought of spending more money on overhead.

"I've been thinking."

"About what?" Jolyn asked distractedly.

"That I could lend you this computer. Just until you can afford a new one."

Jolyn's head came slowly up. She squinted at her mother. "But don't you need it?"

"We can manage without it for a while."

"I really appreciate the offer, Mom, but no. We'll squeak by using my laptop until I can swing an upgrade."

"If you're sure." Dottie pushed her reading glasses up her nose. The next second, her fingers were flying across the keyboard.

Jolyn smiled. For all her mother's quirks, she liked working with her. They were a good team. And while nothing formal had been said, they both assumed Dottie would come with her to the new office on a part-time basis.

As long as her mother's health permitted. Jolyn tapped her pencil on the table, recalling the latest in what had become a long line of frustrations played out over the course of the last five days.

As promised, Dottie had placed a call to her doctor on the Monday, getting the full scoop on her suspicious-looking lumps. The doctor was quick to assure her that "suspicious" didn't mean "cancer." A biopsy was required for an accurate diagnosis.

Today was Friday and Dottie's doctor had only that morning scheduled her procedure. After more than a month of stalling, she'd finally agreed to take the next step and had been waylaid because of a missing document.

Tuesday morning had launched a flurry of communications back and forth between Dottie, her doctor's office, Pineville General Hospital and the insurance company. Jolyn considered herself something of an expert in dealing with insurance companies but even she couldn't budge the HMO mountain.

Yesterday, Dottie had finally located the missing document and faxed it to the insurance company. Not an hour ago, her doctor called to confirm and to give her preop instructions. The hospital would admit her Monday morning at 7:00 a.m. If all went well, she'd be released that afternoon.

Her parents were planning to drive to Pineville on Sunday and stay overnight with Steven and his girlfriend in their new house. Jolyn would leave Monday morning, meeting up with Steven at the hospital right before surgery so they could sit with their father.

Tension in the Sutherland home had reached an all-time high. Keeping busy helped relieve it. One more reason Jolyn was glad for her mother's assistance.

The printer whirred to life and spat out the bid Dottie had typed. She scanned it before getting up and walking it over to Jolyn.

"Thanks, Mom. I'll drop this off to them first thing in the morning."

"What about Chase's final billing?" her mother asked, sitting in the chair adjacent to Jolyn.

"I'm taking that, too. I want to go over it one more time tonight. Make sure I haven't missed anything."

There'd been several changes to the scope of work during construction causing Jolyn to adjust her price. Though she and Chase had discussed the changes in advance, she didn't want to inadvertently overcharge him.

"You two getting along okay?"

"Yeah, why?" Jolyn asked hesitantly, aware that she and Chase had created a stir at the dance on Saturday with their mysterious absence and public hand holding.

"Just wondering."

Her mother seldom just wondered. Sensing she was on a fishing expedition, Jolyn kept her tone light. "I haven't seen him since Wednesday when we did a final walk-through of the clinic."

As it frequently did when reminded of Chase, her mind drifted to their last kiss, a brief but heady stolen moment at the entrance to his clinic. She missed him terribly and couldn't wait for tomorrow.

Construction was officially complete as of yesterday when Mike finished the final punch-list items and the building inspector signed the temporary certificate of occupancy. Jolyn alternated between elation and disappointment. She'd grown accustomed to being at Chase's place nearly every day.

He still had a lot to do on his end before he was ready to open for business. He had veterinarian and office equipment to install and test, supplies to inventory and store, a computer system to set up and specialized software to load, not to mention the all-important soliciting of patients.

"I saw the invitation to his open house," Dottie said. "I can't believe it's tomorrow. They aren't wasting any time."

Mandy and Elizabeth had ridden their bikes all over town, personally delivering the invitations to everyone. Pets and their owners were welcome. Refreshments, for both humans and animals, would be served.

"I understand the open house was Anita's idea. And it's a cute one."

Blue Ridge had never had a small-animal veterinarian practice before. Anyone seeking treatment for their four-legged companions took them to Pineville. Out of necessity, some of the residents had learned to care for their own animals and didn't much see the need for a vet. It was Chase's goal to change their way of thinking.

"I assume you'll be going to the open house," Dottie said.

"Of course. Early, in fact. Just in case there's a last-minute repair."

Chase had also insisted Jolyn stay for the entire afternoon. He was convinced that once people saw firsthand the quality of her work, jobs would come pouring in.

She'd be returning on Sunday, as well. Not for the clinic, but for Mandy's birthday party. The little girl had invited Jolyn when she'd delivered the flyer for the open house. Jolyn had promptly accepted. While the gesture might seem small to some, Jolyn knew it was a big step for Mandy. Hopefully the party would also help to keep Jolyn from worrying about her mother's surgery.

"This looks great, Mom." Jolyn put the bid in a manila file folder and set it aside for the morning.

Her mother didn't leave her seat right away. "I noticed you and Chase were pretty friendly at the dance the other night."

Her *and* twenty or thirty of their friends and neighbors. Though no one had witnessed Jolyn and Chase's scorching kiss behind the officials' booth, word had spread with the swiftness of a raging brushfire. Since they couldn't stop the gossip, they'd agreed to ignore it. Dottie hadn't mentioned the dance all week—probably because she was busy battling her insurance company. Jolyn couldn't help but wonder why her mother was bringing it up now.

"We've always gotten along well," she answered.

"Especially well of late." After a brief pause, Dottie came right out with it. "Are you two involved?"

"No, we're not."

"Oh. I thought maybe—"

"Not yet," Jolyn clarified.

"So, you might."

"We haven't decided."

She considered every answer before she gave it, not yet ready to divulge details to her mother. She'd told Chase her family problem would be resolved on Monday. Because of the glitch with the insurance company, that had turned out not to be the case. He hadn't pressured her when she explained there'd been a delay, but then he was having a busy week himself what with the open house tomorrow and Mandy's birthday on Sunday.

"Is Chase holding back because of me?" Dottie asked.

"Actually, I'm the reluctant one."

"Honey, you must know I don't want to interfere with your happiness." Dottie leaned forward, her elbows resting on the table, her expression earnest.

"You might not *want* to, but *will* you?"

"A person's outlook changes when they realize they may not have long to live." Her mouth curved in a philosophical frown. "You haven't told Chase about the lumps, have you?"

"No, of course not."

Jolyn's mother had sworn the family to silence. "That's good."

"I'm not sure why you're being so secretive. You have nothing to be ashamed of."

"Once people find out you have cancer, that's all they ever talk about. And we decided not to dwell on the negative."

"Talking doesn't have to be negative."

"I'm not ready," Dottie said resolutely. "No more decisions until after the biopsy."

"Decisions?" There was something odd in the way her mother said the word.

"Yes." Rising, Dottie went back to her chair at the computer station. "I've done a lot of soul-searching this week. If the biopsy comes back negative, I won't bother Chase about the DNA testing ever again."

"Really?"

"But if it doesn't—"

"It will." Jolyn cut in before she could finish.

"If it doesn't," Dottie repeated, "if I have breast cancer, I don't know what I'm going to do."

"Mom."

"I just hate the thought of leaving this world without that little girl knowing I'm her grandmother."

"You aren't the only one with something important at stake here."

"I'm the only one who might have cancer."

If her mother could be blunt, so could Jolyn. "Dying doesn't give you the right to break up a loving family."

Dottie had no comeback to that.

CHASE LIFTED the X-ray film and clipped it to a wall-mounted light panel. Anita stood beside him, and together they analyzed the image.

"What do you think?" he asked.

"It doesn't look good." She gave a solemn shake of her head. "Not good at all."

"Hmm," Chase concurred thoughtfully. "Pennies, I say. Three of them."

"Definitely pennies." Anita tapped the film with the tip of a pencil. "You can see Lincoln's head here."

They both turned around. Only Chase spoke. "Ma'am, I am sorry to have to tell you this, but Raggedy Ann has swallowed three pennies. We'll have to operate or she could die."

"Oh, Daddy." Mandy rolled her eyes. "She's a doll. She can't swallow anything."

"Then how do you explain the pennies?" Hard as it was for him, he kept a straight face.

"They're in her pocket." Mandy grabbed the doll off the X-ray table and dug in the front pocket of its apron. "See." She fished out three coins and held them in the flat of her palm for his inspection.

"Huh." Chase scratched his head. "How do you suppose those got in there?"

Mandy's my-father-is-so-dumb-sometimes expression said it all.

Anita broke into laughter. "Your X-ray machine seems to be working perfectly."

"Like a charm." Chase squinted one eye at Mandy. "I'm not so sure about Raggedy Ann. We may have to take a second X ray."

"No." Mandy clutched the precious toy to her chest.

They'd used the doll to give the X-ray machine a test run. Chase would have favored a live subject over a stuffed one, but Buzz and Lickety weren't being cooperative. Like many pets, they'd developed a distinct dislike of veterinary clinics, even when the clinic belonged to their owner. With the open house scheduled to start in an hour, Chase didn't want to stress the dogs out. They needed to be on their best behavior for the canine, feline, feathered and reptilian guests expected to attend.

A vehicle, big by the sound of the engine, pulled up to the clinic entrance.

"I hope that's the caterers." Anita flew out of the examination room. She'd singlehandedly put together the entire open house, for which Chase was truly thankful. He commended himself again for his excellent eye when it came to choosing an assistant.

"Can I help?" Mandy ran after Anita to meet the truck.

The caterer was actually Harold Sage, owner of Sage's Bar and Grill. He was remarkably talented in the kitchen and had embraced the challenge of creating hors d'oeuvres for both people and pets.

Chase straightened the film of Raggedy Ann, leaving the light on so when guests asked him about the X-ray machine, he could explain using show and tell.

"You ready for the big day?" a familiar voice asked.

"Just about." He spun around to see Jolyn standing in the doorway. Whatever else he'd intended to say fled his mind at the sight of her. Slack jawed and tongue tied, he stared, taking a long moment to fully appreciate her appearance. "You're wearing a dress."

"Yeah." She plucked at the silky folds of fabric, her mouth pursed. "Too fancy do you think? I could go home and change." She let go of the skirt, and it floated down to fall softly around her legs.

Legs!

"Don't do that." He hadn't seen her in anything but jeans since the day she came home and was in no hurry for her to revert back to her old habits. This one suited him just fine.

The hem of the floral sundress covered her knees but only by an inch at most. Enough bare calves and shoulders were exposed to give him a testosterone rush the likes of which he hadn't felt in years. Brightly painted toenails peeked out from a pair of slim, high-heeled sandals, so different from the athletic shoes or cowboy boots she typically wore. Her hair had been curled and styled and pinned back with a simple, yet elegant, clasp.

"You look great." Only the presence of Anita, Mandy and Harold in the reception area kept his feet glued to the floor. If they were alone, he'd…

"Thanks." She smiled shyly. "Probably not the best outfit for a construction company owner to wear."

"It's *exactly* the best outfit to wear." He must have been ogling her pretty hard because her cheeks turned an appealing shade of pink.

"I should go help set up the food." She retreated a step.

"Not yet." Kissing her was preferable but with so many people in the vicinity, he'd have to settle for a simple, fleeting touch. He came out from behind the examination table and strode toward her. In the doorway, he stopped to gaze down at her. "I've missed you." He raised his hand and stroked the line of her jaw with his knuckles.

Her laugh was soft and feminine and utterly enchanting. "We just saw each other yesterday."

"That was business." He stepped closer. "And not what I was referring to."

He drew an invisible line down the side of her neck and then along the length of her collarbone. She tilted her head, shivered slightly and held her breath until he stopped. Not by choice. Any more of this, of her response to him, and he'd do something drastic. Wouldn't his guests just love that?

Backing up a step, then two, he leaned a hip against the counter and fought for control. He won. Barely. "Are things any better at home?"

"Yes and no." She sighed and pushed a strand of gold-streaked hair away from her face.

He waited for her to elaborate. She'd told him at the dance last Saturday that the situation at home would be resolved on Monday. It hadn't been. And it was obvious to anyone who knew the Sutherlands that the lack of resolution was wearing on them.

"We've made progress, at least," she said. "And should know more this week."

"Good."

"Knowing may or may not be good." She swallowed and cleared her throat, visibly struggling to rein in her emotions.

"Oh, sweetheart." Screw proprieties. He went to her and put an arm around her, pulling her flush against him.

"Sorry." She sniffed. "It's been a rough week."

"No need to apologize."

"My parents had a particularly unpleasant blowup this morning."

Jolyn rarely discussed her family with him. That she mentioned something so personal showed—more than the kisses they'd shared—how their relationship was changing.

"Parents fight on occasion. And it's never easy on the kids. Even when those kids are adults."

"They've made up already. But it was tough going for an hour there."

"I'm glad."

"I should freshen up."

"If you need anything, call me. I'm a good listener."

"I know you are," she said and pressed a hand to his chest.

That small touch was enough to break Chase's resolve. At the exact moment he decided kissing her would be an excellent idea after all, Anita and Mandy thundered down the hall. Chase and Jolyn sprang apart like a pair of guilty lovers.

Judging from her happy, carefree expression, Mandy didn't appear to have noticed anything amiss. No surprise there.

Between the open house today and her birthday party tomorrow, she was wrapped up in her own little world.

Anita was a different matter. She'd clearly seen Chase and Jolyn on the verge of locking lips. However, the only thing she said was, "You might want to come out here. Folks are starting to arrive."

Smart woman.

Chapter Thirteen

"These are darn tasty." Russell Meyer plucked an hors d'oeuvre from one of the many trays set out in the reception area and popped it into his mouth.

"How many have you had?" Jolyn hid a smirk.

"Three. I love sardines. My wife won't let me have them," he whispered. "She hates the smell of fish."

"You do know those are cat hors d'oeuvres?"

"Cat?" His eyes bulged.

"Yes." Jolyn chuckled.

"Will they hurt me?"

"I don't think so."

"Whew!" He wiped his eyebrow. "Because I wouldn't want to get sick." He stole another kitty treat, swallowing it whole.

"Mr. Meyer!"

He cast a worried glance over her shoulder. "Don't say anything."

A second later, his wife, Barbara, joined them. An English bulldog with a severe underbite trailed at the end of the leash Mrs. Meyer held. The dog jumped up on Mr. Meyer's leg, sniffed his hand and started licking his fingers.

"Behave, Sir Adorable." Barbara shook a disapproving finger at the dog and then her husband. "Russell, don't let him do that."

He flashed Jolyn a guilty look before pushing the dog down.

"Jolyn, this clinic is just wonderful." Mrs. Meyer linked arms with Jolyn. "Seriously, I had no idea you were so talented."

"Thank you." Had the backhanded compliment come from anyone besides the self-absorbed but sweet-underneath-it-all coowner of the Blue Ridge Inn, Jolyn might have been offended.

"You do know we're expanding the inn." She spoke in the same conspiratorial whisper her husband had used not two minutes earlier.

"No, I didn't."

"Tell her about it, dear."

She elbowed her husband, who was eyeing a tray of bacon-wrapped chicken livers intended for the likes of Sir Adorable, not him. Jolyn considered suggesting he try the baked brie rounds instead.

"Ah, yeah." He returned his attention to Jolyn. "A new wing with three additional rooms *and* an inground swimming pool."

"Swimming pool?"

Jolyn could count on one hand the number of people in Blue Ridge who owned above-ground circular pools. In-ground ones were unheard of.

"We'd like you to bid the job," Mrs. Meyer said determinedly. "Wouldn't we, Russell?"

"Why, yes." He recovered quickly from his wife's obviously unexpected announcement.

Outwardly, Jolyn smiled politely. Inwardly, she was jumping up and down like a maniac. This could be *the* job, the one to generate enough income to carry her company for the coming months. Quickly running numbers in her head, she estimated the job to be twice, if not three times, the size of Chase's clinic.

"I'd like very much to bid your job," she said in her best professional voice, cautioning herself to stay calm.

Just because she quoted them a price didn't mean she'd get

the job. So many things could go awry, especially in a project this size. Financing could fall through. Permits could be denied because of zoning restrictions. An engineering report could come back showing the ground unsuitable for a swimming pool.

And there was always the chance another contractor might underbid her. The Meyers were intelligent business people. They would obtain more than one bid, and loyalty to the hometown girl only went so far.

"When are you looking to start construction?" she inquired.

"Soon," Mrs. Meyer answered. "Two months at the very most. We'd like to be finished before December."

"We're always booked to capacity during the holidays," Mr. Meyer explained. "And could use those rooms."

"We'll call you the first of the week. Set up an appointment." Mrs. Meyer tugged on Sir Adorable's leash, and the dog obediently ceased sniffing a poodle's hind end.

"Would you like my business card?" Jolyn reached for one from the stack on the counter. Chase had insisted she put them out, and she couldn't help noticing that half were gone.

"Yes. Thank you." Mr. Meyer took the card from Jolyn's hand and while his wife's back was turned, swiped another sardine appetizer. Swallowing it whole, he grinned at Jolyn, then he and his wife and Sir Adorable moved on to continue mingling.

A group of excited children gathered around a table where Mandy was distributing coupons for half off on a first visit—something which pleased the children's parents—and free goldfish in small plastic containers, which didn't please the parents nearly so much.

As Jolyn walked from room to room, she was constantly stopped and engaged in conversation. She admired pets, most of them dogs but also a kitten that hadn't stopped yowling since it arrived, a two-foot iguana, a parrot that rode on its owner's arm and sang "Somewhere Over the Rainbow" when prompted and a pair of very nervous hamsters. She also accepted compliments on the construction and got two leads on nice, albeit small, jobs.

More than once she looked across a room or down the hall to catch Chase's dark brown eyes watching her. His smile seemed to say *This is your party, too. Your celebration. Enjoy it.*

She *was* enjoying herself, reveling in her accomplishments and the realization of a dream come true. For the first time in days, she didn't worry about her mother's health. With her enjoyment came a sense that everything would eventually resolve itself. A foolish idea perhaps, but Jolyn didn't care. She felt too good, too optimistic, to let anything spoil her happiness.

Unfortunately, the feeling didn't last. When she returned to the reception area, it was to see the latest guests arrive. At the sight of her mother and father coming through the door, her mood went from elated to anxious in the blink of an eye.

CHASE CAUGHT SIGHT of Jolyn heading back into the reception area. He'd have liked to follow and spend a minute with her but they were constantly surrounded by people and, more so in Chase's case, pets. Which was a good thing and the whole reason he'd thrown the open house. From all appearances, they were both in for a slew of new customers.

He was impressed with the way she handled herself, her poise and charm. Jolyn had really and truly come into her own during her time away. As a kid and later a teenager, she'd been constantly overshadowed by SherryAnne's larger-than-life personality. Chase didn't regret his marriage. If not for SherryAnne, he wouldn't have Mandy. But he wasn't sorry they'd divorced when they had and that Jolyn, by some minor miracle, was also single.

"Your clinic is beautiful."

The owner of the Double S Ranch and matriarch of the Shaughnessy family offered her hand to Chase. "We're going to miss you at the ranch."

"I'll still come out. Just not as often."

"Anita appears a capable sort. I suppose we'll manage with her." "Capable sort" was high praise coming from Mrs. Shaughnessy.

"You can still call me anytime for anything."

"I will hold you to that." Her smile was tight but not unfriendly.

He had nothing but the utmost respect for his oldest and dearest customer. The Double S was one of the best-run ranches in the area, thanks entirely to its owner, who, in her late seventies, still rode daily, overseeing each and every detail of the ranch's operation.

"Speaking of Anita, where is she?" Mrs. Shaughnessy inquired.

"I'm not sure. She was here just a minute ago." With Mike glued to her side as he'd been all afternoon.

"Daddy. Daddy." Mandy burst into the surgery, her gaze darting in every direction.

"Over here." To Mrs. Shaughnessy, Chase said, "Excuse me, please."

"If you run into Anita, tell her I'm looking for her."

Spoken like a true queen, thought Chase. "I will."

"Can I spend the night at 'Lizabeth's house?" Mandy asked, throwing herself at Chase and hugging him around the waist.

"I supposed. Is it all right with her mother?"

"Yes."

"What about your birthday party tomorrow?"

"I'll be back early. I promise."

"Ten o'clock. We still have a lot to do to get ready."

"Okay."

They weren't having many people over. Family mostly.

Susan, Joseph, Chase's cousin Gage, Gage's wife, Aubrey, and Hannah, of course. Plus four or five of Mandy's friends. Oh, and Jolyn. Chase was pleased that Mandy had invited her, and hoped this meant Mandy had become more accepting of his growing relationship with Jolyn.

"Which means no staying up late tonight watching movies," he warned his daughter.

"I'll bring 'Lizabeth with me. She can help, too."

Chase doubted that. Whenever the two girls were together, they fooled around more than they applied themselves. But he couldn't refuse Mandy. It was her birthday, after all, and he was glad to see her so happy. She'd probably remain so as long as SherryAnne didn't call again.

"I'm going to go tell 'Lizabeth." Mandy sprinted around a corner and was instantly lost in the crowd.

Chase went in search of Jolyn, but was stopped by yet another guest who asked to see how the anesthesia machine worked. He didn't escape for a full ten minutes.

Finding his way to the reception area at last, he noticed while the open house was scheduled to end in thirty minutes, the crowd had yet to thin. He'd never imagined the day would be such a resounding success. For about the tenth time that afternoon, he stepped on a future patient's paw.

"Sorry, guy." He scratched the dog's head fondly, smiled at the owner and continued looking for Jolyn.

And then he found her. She was standing in a corner talking to Sam Green, the owner of Mountain View Real Estate, where his Aunt Susan worked part-time. From the looks of it, their conversation was going well. Sam could be a valuable contact for Jolyn, referring clients in need of home repairs or new home construction to her.

Chase decided not to intrude. He was thinking about going to the counter and nabbing a bite to eat when a voice from behind stopped him.

"Congratulations on your new clinic, Chase. It's very impressive."

He turned, slowly, to greet his newest guest.

"Dottie." He didn't acknowledge her compliment.

The invitation to the open house had gone out to everyone in town. He'd excluded no one. And even if he had restricted his guest list, Jolyn's parents would have been on it. She'd built the clinic and would want her family to see it. Out of respect for her, Chase could tolerate her mother's presence.

"Jolyn did an incredible job," Dottie said, lifting a plastic cup of lemonade to her lips and taking a sip.

"Yes, she did."

"I wish you the best of luck." Her hand shook when she lowered the cup, the ice cubes rattling against the sides. Nerves? Chase didn't think so. Dottie was made of iron.

"I'm proud of her."

"You should be."

She'd lost weight. And there were dark circles under her eyes. Chase could see other small changes now that he was up close. He almost felt sorry for her. *Almost.* To his mind, she'd brought her problems on herself. She could, if she chose, leave him and Mandy alone. Her husband and children were content to do just that.

"I wish Steven had been able to come down from Pineville today. He had to work."

Was her remark innocent or deliberate? Chase was never entirely sure with Dottie. At least he now knew for certain that Steven wasn't at the open house. That took a load off his mind.

"If you'll excuse me, Dottie." He'd done his part, made nice with Jolyn's mother, endured the passing glances of everyone in the room who knew their past and had to be dying of curiosity.

"Just a minute." She laid a hand on his arm.

Chase tensed, stared hard at her hand and fought to contain his dislike and distrust. This wasn't the time or place for another confrontation with her. From across the room, he saw Jolyn weaving through the crowd toward them. She must also have decided not to make a scene because she stopped short just before reaching them.

"I don't want to ruin your life," Dottie said, speaking softly so that only Chase heard. "You're a good man, a good father."

"Then why are you?" he demanded with more bitterness than he'd intended.

"I admit my motives were entirely selfish at first. I guess they still are." The ice cubes in her cup rattled again, and she used two hands in an effort to quell the shaking. "But you may find my...current reasons more sympathetic."

Who did she think she was, coming to his house, suggesting he of all people would sympathize with her trying to take his daughter away from him? The fury he'd been keeping at bay suddenly erupted. "It'll be a cold day in hell when that happens."

Dottie didn't retreat from his verbal attack. Neither did she retaliate, as usual.

"I'll let you know when I get there," she said simply, then walked away from Chase and kept walking until she was out the clinic door.

"I HOPE MY MOTHER didn't upset you."

Chase willed himself to relax, and dismissed Jolyn's concerns with a smile. "If anything, she was quite civil." And she had been. Even her parting remark was delivered without venom.

I'll let you know when I get there.

Chase had no idea what Dottie meant by her cryptic comment, other than to make him feel guilty, and he was resolved not to ask Jolyn. She'd received nothing but positive feedback on the clinic from guests, and several encouraging leads. Rather than spoil her high, he played down his confrontation with her mother.

"She left without saying goodbye," Jolyn mused.

"I think she was tired."

They were going from room to room, emptying trash into big green garbage bags. The last guest had finally left shortly after seven. Chase had tried to send Jolyn, Anita and Mike home, saying he'd clean up tomorrow, but they'd all insisted on staying and helping. Anita and Mike were busy transferring leftover food into containers and taking them to the refrigerator in the house. Chase didn't think he'd have to buy any food—human or dog—for a week at least.

"Don't worry. I'm sure your mother's fine." He reached for Jolyn's hand and brought it to his mouth. They'd had so little physical contact the last few days. Chase was desperate for a taste of her. Even a small one.

And it would be small if Anita and Mike had anything to do with it. The entrance door opened with a bang, letting Chase and Jolyn know their respective employees had returned. Later, he vowed to himself. He'd finagle a few minutes alone with Jolyn before she left.

"Hey, there you are."

Anita poked her head into Chase's office, where he and Jolyn had wound up on their trash collecting sweep.

"Hey." Chase didn't let go of Jolyn's hand. Why bother? Anita had already caught them carrying on earlier.

"Food's all put away," she said. "Would it be okay if Mike and I split? Or do you need some more help?"

Fate, it seemed, was on his side tonight after all.

"I think we can manage." Chase strived for a nonchalance he didn't feel. In another minute, he'd be alone with Jolyn. Truly alone. And he planned to take full advantage of the privacy.

"You sure?" Anita's inquisitive gaze lighted first on Jolyn, then Chase.

"Very sure." Chase's steely stare let her know her job was on the line if she didn't beat it out of there pronto.

"See you Monday, then."

"Hey." He stopped her before she disappeared. "Thanks for your help. I couldn't have done this alone."

"Job security." She cranked up her thousand-watt smile. "I kind of like it here. And if you do well, I get to stick around."

"Mike have anything to do with it?"

"He's a definite perk."

Chase chuckled.

In the next second, she was gone.

He arched an eyebrow at Jolyn. Though he ached to kiss her, to take her in his arms and again explore the soft curves and tantalizing angles of her body, he hesitated, allowing her to make the first move. Or not. In light of her recent family issues, she might have decided a relationship with him wasn't worth the problems that came with it. He'd understand. Sort of. Okay, maybe not understand as much as respect her wishes.

It was hell being a gentleman.

"I guess the cat's officially out of the bag," she said, arranging and rearranging the items on Chase's desk.

"About us?"

"I was referring to Anita and Mike."

"Ah." He threw the last of the trash into the garbage bag and knotted the plastic ties.

"I think we're last week's news."

"Does it bother you?"

"What?" She laughed. "That people have someone else to gossip about besides us? Hardly."

"That people were gossiping about us in the first place."

"I'd venture to say my family's been the topic of many a dinner conversation these past couple of weeks. An honor I'd gladly relinquish." She smiled, a warm, genuine and sexy smile directed right at him. "But no, I don't mind the gossip nearly as much as I thought I might."

"No?"

She shook her head and shifted, her movements slow, languid and very inviting. The dress rustled, swished, then re-settled around her bare legs.

Steady, boy, Chase warned himself. He couldn't tell if she was enticing him on purpose or not. His body didn't know the difference and responded with a will of its own.

"Good." Forgetting all about his commitment to let her make the first move, he came around the side of the desk.

She met him with open arms, and the eagerness with which she slid into his embrace left no doubt she wanted him as much as he wanted her.

Lifting her by the waist, he set her on the desk, knocking over the items she'd so carefully arranged. His fingers slid beneath the hem of her dress, discovering a creamy expanse of smooth thigh that turned need into an insatiable hunger. She wrapped one calf around the back of his knee and proceeded to incite his desire to even further heights by scraping her nails up and down the muscles of his back.

If one of them didn't come to their senses soon they'd... what? Make love? Hell, yes. It was what he wanted. Jolyn, too, or so her questing fingers and inability to draw a decent breath seemed to indicate.

He pulled back, gazed into her face and momentarily lost the power of speech. It was then that he realized the incredible depths of his feelings for her. No woman had ever struck him dumb before.

"What's wrong?" she asked.

"Nothing," he said, finding his voice. He smoothed the worry lines from her forehead with tender strokes of his fingers. "Let's go into the house."

She cradled his face in her hands and pressed a light kiss to his lips, letting him know she returned his feelings. "Yes. Let's."

Chase eased Jolyn off the desk and into his arms where, if he had anything to say about it, she'd spend every minute of the night—and many more nights to come.

Chapter Fourteen

"Would you like something to drink? A glass of wine maybe?"

"No, thanks." Jolyn stood in Chase's kitchen, just inside the back door.

She'd visited the Raintree home often while they were growing up. The kitchen and living room. Not once had she ventured into the bedroom area. The very idea of it felt somehow forbidden.

And exciting.

"Have something if you'd like," she told him. "Don't let me stop you."

"Fine. If you insist." His arm snaked around her waist, and he lifted her against him. Sampling her lips, he said, "Much better than wine."

"I agree."

She stood on tiptoes, sinking deeper into his embrace and feeling headier than if she'd drunk an entire bottle of the finest champagne.

Chase must have been as impatient as she to make love because he stooped and caught her behind the knees, picked her up in his arms and carried her through the house.

He kicked open the master bedroom door, entered and gently set her down on the bed. Skimming his lips lightly across hers, he said, "Wait here, I'll be right back."

Seconds later light poured from the doorway of the adjoining bathroom. The sound of a medicine cabinet being opened reached her ears. He was probably getting protection. Good. One of them, at least, was thinking ahead.

Chase returned, leaving the door cracked open. A tiny sliver of light illuminated his broad-shouldered form from behind as he moved toward the bed. He stopped next to where Jolyn lay and tossed something onto the nightstand.

Condoms, she guessed. And more than one. He really was thinking ahead.

Then, he started to undress.

He began with his belt and shirt. Both items landed in a heap on the carpeted floor. Jolyn watched him, mesmerized. The well-defined muscles of his naked shoulders, arms and chest were a tribute to his active life. She would have liked to skim her hands over the enticing ripples and planes but that would come in time. For now, she much preferred to watch.

With each article of clothing he removed, he looked at her, studying her reaction, and only when she let out a soft sigh did he continue. Jolyn held her breath as long as possible, not wanting to hurry the process. No man had ever undressed for her before, and she liked it.

The slight smile that had been playing around the corners of his mouth vanished when he unsnapped his jeans. Hand poised on the zipper, he went still. She rose onto her knees, the mattress dipping beneath her weight.

He wouldn't stop. Not now. She'd never forgive him if he did.

"I have to see you, all of you," he said, his voice rough with need.

Her hands shook slightly as she pulled the dress over her head. Still kneeling, she faced him in her skimpy bra and even skimpier panties.

A low grumble of appreciation emanated from deep in his chest.

Letting her gaze wander the length of him from head to toe, she knew exactly how he felt.

With a quick jerk of his hand, he unzipped his jeans and stepped out of them. The cotton boxer briefs he wore did nothing to hide his erection.

"Your turn." He pointed to her bra.

She undid each hook and slipped off her bra, dangling it over the side of the bed for several seconds before letting go and sinking back onto the mattress.

"You're so beautiful."

His words filled her with warmth.

And as she watched him admire her body, the warmth inside her changed to the scorching heat of passion. Under his gaze her nipples beaded to taut buds. The sensation was exquisitely erotic, unlike anything she'd ever felt.

Sliding his thumbs into the waistband of his boxer briefs, he slowly eased them down his lean hips until he stood before her, unashamed and undeniably aroused.

"You're wrong," Jolyn whispered, helpless to take her eyes off him, desperate to touch him and feel the hard, masculine length of him flush against her. "You're the one who's beautiful."

He came to her then, and she lay back on the bed, opening herself to him. With one knee on the mattress, he reached for her panties and gently tugged them down her legs, his fingers caressing her skin.

And then there were no more barriers between them, physical or emotional. Whatever problems they had to overcome were pushed aside, left for another day.

Chase propped himself up on one arm, leaning over her to kiss her fiercely, then running a hand along her hip, up her stomach, over her breast. His thumb and forefinger closed around a nipple, squeezed and tugged softly until she arched into him. Then he lowered his head and took the nipple into his mouth.

His lips and tongue were wet, hot and highly skilled. Sifting her fingers through his hair, she pulled him closer. He moved to her other breast, and this time when he sucked on her nipple, there was a greater urgency about him as if his control was starting to slip.

He rolled onto his side and, locking an arm around her, tugged her to him. Nudging her legs open, his hand sought and found her feminine folds. His fingertips glided over her, gently probed, then entered her with less restraint. A low hiss of satisfaction escaped his lips when he found her damp and ready for him.

Through a fog of desire, she realized he was leaning on one elbow, watching her in the semidarkness. Such intimate scrutiny should have bothered her, but it didn't. Her languid movements and soft sighs of pleasure were obviously turning him on, and she was turned on by the very powerful effect she had on him.

It was enough to send her toppling over the edge. The fall couldn't have been any sweeter, any more satisfying, and was well worth the years of waiting and dreaming.

"Mmm. That was…oh, wow." She stretched and rolled onto her side to snuggle against him, her fingers exploring the patch of hair on his chest.

"Pretty much how I feel, too." His grin was smug, and why not?

When her hand wandered lower, over the flat muscles of his stomach, he sucked in a sharp breath. Emboldened by his response, she pushed him onto his back and trapped him with a leg thrown over his.

"Turnabout's fair play," she said, nibbling his ear while her hand closed around his erection.

Chase's response was a ragged groan.

He lasted only a minute before he pushed her hand aside and grabbed one of the condoms off the nightstand. Quickly donning it, he lifted her by the waist and set her on top of him so that she straddled his middle.

She didn't take him inside her just yet. Rocking her hips, she slid back and forth over him, her slick heat a perfect match for his hardness.

Pulling her down to him, he lifted a breast in his hand and drew the nipple into his mouth, teasing it with his tongue. Jolyn's determination to draw out the foreplay cracked. With a thready moan, she elevated her hips, positioned him beneath her and came down fast, taking him deep inside her.

Chase swore and went utterly still, then began thrusting into her with strong, swift strokes. Moments later he came, groaning her name and clinging to her as if she might suddenly leave him and not return.

As if there was any possibility of that happening.

JOLYN BLINKED HER EYES, yawned and stretched. Seeing Chase, she smiled shyly and murmured, "What are you doing?"

"Watching you."

And he had been for quite some time, still in a state of disbelief. He'd spent half the night having the best sex of his life and the other half sleeping with Jolyn cradled in his arms. He couldn't remember the last time he'd felt so happy.

She was an incredible lover. She'd surprised and delighted him with her sensual nature and lack of inhibition. The memory of the hours they'd spent exploring each other's bodies, touching and tasting every intimate place, incited a fresh hunger in him.

Jolyn peered over his shoulder at the digital clock. "Oh, my gosh. It's after eight already."

"We have time." He cupped her hip with his hand, then caressed her thigh with long, intimate strokes.

She pushed a tousled lock of hair from her face. "I'm a mess."

"You're gorgeous."

Lying naked in his bedsheets, her golden hair spread atop his pillow, she'd never looked more stunning. If she doubted him, she need only move her leg three inches to feel his swelling erection.

"I might be talked into taking a quick shower with you."

He chuckled, charmed by her brashness and admittedly relieved. There would be no morning-after discomfort. He'd worried about that as he watched her sleep.

"A shower sounds good," he said, dipping his hand between her legs. "But not yet."

Despite Jolyn's claim that it was getting late, they didn't hurry, savoring a joining that was somehow more tender than those of the previous night. Chase hadn't been with a woman since his divorce, but he didn't attribute his powerful response to—and insatiable hunger for—this woman to his long abstinence.

She, and only she, was responsible for that.

He wasn't sure where their relationship was headed after today, only that it was headed somewhere.

Showering and then dressing, they went out to the kitchen.

"Coffee?" Chase asked.

"One cup. I really need to get home."

"You could stay. The birthday party starts in…" He checked the clock on the microwave. "Six hours."

"I have Mandy's gift at home. And I'd like to change. Everyone coming today saw me wearing this dress yesterday." She absently smoothed the skirt. "My parents will be wondering where I am, too."

She'd called them the previous night from her cell phone. Chase hadn't listened to the conversation, knew only that she'd given them some explanation for not coming home.

He toasted English muffins while the coffee brewed. Anything to keep Jolyn with him a few minutes longer. She did need to leave soon, though, or they'd risk being caught by Mandy.

Chase didn't quite know how his daughter would react to him dating. He'd feel better easing her into the idea rather than springing it on her all at once by having her walk in on him and Jolyn enjoying breakfast together. Mandy might only be turning nine, but she was wise enough to figure out more was going on than a postconstruction meeting.

"You up for dinner one night this week?" he asked. They sat at the kitchen table, drinking coffee and eating muffin halves.

"A date?" Her eyebrows shot up.

"Yeah. I was thinking spaghetti Wednesday at Sage's."

"Um…"

"We could take Mandy. Make it a family outing."

"If we went to dinner at Sage's, even with Mandy, everyone in town would jump to conclusions."

"Are you okay with that?" He was, but he shouldn't take it for granted she felt the same.

"I am."

"You don't sound a hundred percent."

Jolyn fiddled with her mug of coffee, turning it in circles. Twice she started to speak only to snap her mouth shut.

"Is it your mother?" he asked.

"Yes."

Chase reached for her hand, folding it inside his and squeezing hard. "We can't let her affect what we have. I won't—"

"She's sick."

"What?"

"Maybe very sick. We don't know yet. She's having outpatient surgery tomorrow. A biopsy." Tears filled Jolyn's eyes.

Chase was speechless. Of all the possibilities he'd considered, serious illness wasn't one of them. Suddenly Dottie's cryptic remark at the open house yesterday made sense. After several seconds, he said, "I'm…sorry. Is there anything I can do?"

"No, but thank you."

"I mean it. I'm not saying what I think you want to hear."

"That's very generous of you considering how my mother's treated you."

"What's wrong with her? Can I ask?"

Jolyn shook her head. "She made me promise not to say anything. I've probably revealed too much as it is."

"How long has she been sick?"

"Five or six weeks, if not longer. She won't say."

"That's when she started to pressure me again about Mandy."

"Which makes sense."

"She didn't look well yesterday at the open house."

"No, she didn't."

"I thought it might be stress. There's been talk around town of trouble."

"We're all under a lot of stress." Jolyn flashed him a brave smile.

"I can't even imagine what you're going through." Chase's parents were in the best of health and enjoying their semiretirement. He always assumed they'd live to an advanced age like his grandparents.

Just how sick was Dottie?

Sick enough that she would come to Chase and demand he have DNA testing done on him and Mandy.

"Is your mother's illness treatable?"

"There's treatment." Jolyn's voice fell to a whisper. "But no guarantee of a cure."

"I'm sorry, honey." Rising, he went to Jolyn, pulled her from her chair and took her in his arms. They held each other, offering and accepting comfort.

"Are you going to the hospital with your mother?"

"Dad's driving her to Pineville this afternoon. I'll go up tomorrow morning. The procedure's scheduled for nine."

"Would you like me to go with you?"

"I can't impose on you like that."

"It's no imposition."

"Yes, it is. You have a new clinic to set up." She laid her head on his chest. "It means a lot to me that you offered. But I think it would be best if you didn't."

He bent and kissed her, gently, lovingly. It was Jolyn who took the kiss to the next level, clutching him with mild desperation. Chase sensed it wasn't sex she needed from him right then, but a physical and emotional connection. He gave it to her.

So caught up were they in their kiss that the sound of the kitchen door opening didn't immediately penetrate the haze surrounding them. When it finally did, Chase panicked.

Mandy! She'd come home early from Elizabeth's.

He broke off the kiss and pushed Jolyn aside. Shielding her behind him, he spun around to confront his daughter, an explanation on the tip of his tongue.

Only it wasn't Mandy who stood just inside the door, suitcase in hand, an unpleasant smile on her face.

"Well," she said, setting her suitcase on the floor and crossing her arms over her chest. "This is unexpected."

"SherryAnne," Chase growled. "What the hell are you doing here?"

Chapter Fifteen

"It's my daughter's birthday," SherryAnne announced. "I was planning to surprise her. Guess I'm the one surprised. Or maybe not." Her eyes narrowed accusingly. "How are you, Jolyn?"

"You should have called," Chase said before Jolyn could answer. He didn't want SherryAnne talking to her, didn't want SherryAnne within ten miles of his house.

"What would have been the fun in that? And speaking of fun, where's my daughter?"

"At a friend's house. She'll be home any minute."

SherryAnne picked up her suitcase and strolled across the kitchen as if she owned the place. "I'll wait."

"Not here you won't." Chase intercepted her.

"Are you saying I'm not welcome here?"

"Yes. That's exactly what I'm saying."

SherryAnne mustered a healthy dose of indignation. "You'd deny me the chance to be with my daughter?"

"Don't try to lay any guilt trips on me. You're the one who hasn't seen Mandy in over a year."

"That wasn't by choice," SherryAnne objected. "Once you won custody—"

"Don't even go there," Chase warned. "You've always had choices."

"Where am I supposed to stay if not here?"

From the corner of his eye, Chase noticed Jolyn retrieving her purse and other things from the counter. He debated between insisting she stay—SherryAnne had no right running her off—and hustling her out the door. Things were bound to get ugly with him and his ex-wife.

"You can stay at the inn," he said to SherryAnne.

"Only if you pay," she answered flippantly. "Seems I'm a little strapped for cash these days."

Chase was a little strapped himself and would be until the new clinic took off, but he'd gladly empty his entire savings account if it kept SherryAnne out of his house.

"Fine. Have the Meyers call me when you check in, and I'll give them my credit card number."

Jolyn squeezed past Chase and mumbled, "I'll see you later."

He waylaid her and stated rather than asked, "You're still coming to Mandy's birthday party."

"That's probably not a good idea."

"No, it's a *fine* idea," SherryAnne said with forced joviality. "Oh, wait." Her gaze went from Jolyn to Chase. "Unless Mandy doesn't know about you two." She tilted her head inquisitively. "Is that it?"

"Don't say anything to her," Chase said, his tone harsh.

SherryAnne put a finger to her lips. "Mum's the word."

Chase didn't believe her. Nothing he'd seen in the last five minutes gave him reason to think his ex-wife had changed.

"I really have to go," Jolyn said.

"Okay." She was understandably uncomfortable, and he didn't feel right about having her witness him and Sherry-Anne hurling insults at each other. "See you in a few hours."

Her small nod didn't fill him with confidence, so he decided to do something about it by planting a soft kiss on her mouth. Jolyn stiffened but didn't retreat. After a few seconds, she placed her hand on his shoulder and increased the pressure of her lips ever so slightly.

"That's my girl," he whispered in her ear when they separated. She hadn't let SherryAnne get to her.

"How sweet," SherryAnne commented as Jolyn went past her.

She stopped and turned to SherryAnne. "I'm glad for Mandy that you're here," she said with a sincerity SherryAnne didn't deserve. "She misses you."

Jolyn may not have intended to stick it to SherryAnne, but her remark accomplished just that.

"Bitch," SherryAnne muttered once the door was shut.

"Why?" Chase demanded. "Because she spoke the truth?"

"I'm not shocked that you two hooked up the second she hit town. She always had a thing for you."

"Is that why you kept me around all those years even when you were tired of me? Because you didn't want your best friend to have me?"

"Oh, please." SherryAnne made a face. "Like I was worried about any competition."

"You should have been." Chase remembered the night he'd kissed Jolyn on her parents' front porch. "I'd have started dating her in a heartbeat."

"Looks like you got your wish," she quipped.

"Don't think you can spoil what Jolyn and I have."

SherryAnne swept past Chase and went to the counter, where she poured herself a cup of coffee without being invited. "I don't want you anymore, Chase."

"For which I thank God every day."

"My, my. Still sore, are we?"

"What do you want, SherryAnne?"

"I'm here for my daughter's birthday."

"Please. Unselfish acts of kindness aren't part of your character."

"Why, I believe I'm offended." She placed a hand over her chest.

"We both know it takes more than a minor dig to offend you."

"My sole motive in coming here is to celebrate my daughter's birthday and to spend a few days with her."

Chase was relieved to hear her visit would only be for a few days. However, he doubted her motives were as pure as she claimed.

"You drove here?" he asked.

"All the way from Oklahoma City." She helped herself to a leftover English muffin.

"Why don't you go check in to the inn and come back when the party starts?"

"Tired of me already?"

He might have answered her if not for the door banging open. Mandy burst into the kitchen, followed closely by the dogs.

"Daddy? Whose truck is that out—" She came to a grinding halt at the sight of SherryAnne. "Mommy!"

"Baby." SherryAnne opened her arms, and Mandy flew into them.

Chase cursed under his breath. So much for getting rid of SherryAnne until the party. But, because he loved his daughter more than he despised his ex-wife, he'd find a way to survive the next few days.

HALFWAY INTO Mandy's birthday party Jolyn began to seriously question her decision to attend.

After the unpleasant scene with SherryAnne that morning, she'd been determined not to let Chase's ex-wife scare her away. He wanted her at the party. Mandy had invited her. But as she sat on a chair in a corner of the patio, watching SherryAnne play games with Mandy and her friends, serve cake and ice cream and visit with Susan and Joseph Raintree as if they were long lost friends, Jolyn felt more and more out of place.

It reminded her too much of high school. Either consciously or unconsciously, they'd fallen into their former roles.

SherryAnne, with her domineering personality, hogged the spotlight, taking charge of everyone and everything. Chase, perhaps because he didn't want to ruin Mandy's birthday, went along with SherryAnne for the most part. Jolyn hung on the outskirts, a part of the activity but not truly involved. She hated it even more than she had eleven years ago. And, just like then, she didn't know what to do about it.

This wasn't how she wanted to spend the day before her mother's surgery. She had intended to go home after a few hours of pleasant distraction and help with any last-minute tasks. Instead, she'd be thinking of SherryAnne, there at Chase's house, digging her claws into him.

It wasn't fair to her mother, who deserved her family's full attention at this crucial time.

"Mind if I sit here?" Chase's cousin, Hannah, didn't wait for an invitation before slipping into the empty chair next to Jolyn. "Nice party."

"Very nice."

"Do you think it's going to rain?" Hannah hitched her chin at the clouds gathering in the northern sky.

"That's what they're saying."

Jolyn didn't know Chase's cousin very well. She'd been just a kid when Jolyn had left to tour with the show. They'd run in to each other off and on during recent weeks, mostly at Chase's clinic. Jolyn didn't sense the same reservation in Hannah she did in his aunt and uncle. If anything, Hannah appeared to approve of Jolyn. At least, as Chase's friend. No one knew that their relationship had changed to…to what?

"Oh, Mandy, baby," SherryAnne trilled at the top of her voice. "Are you going to let your father get away with that?"

She clung to Chase's arm and laughed up into his face.

"She's a piece of work, isn't she?" Hannah said, shaking her head in disgust.

Jolyn held her tongue. This was Chase's family, and they were notoriously tight-knit. They might not like Sherry-Anne but neither were they keen on welcoming Jolyn into the fold.

"It's cool," Hannah went on. "You don't have to answer. I like that you're loyal to Chase."

Loyalty wasn't what motivated Jolyn. "I'm glad Sherry-Anne came back."

Hannah gave Jolyn a dubious look. "You are?"

"For Mandy."

"Of course. Not because she's your best friend."

"*Former* best friend."

"There's the tigress I knew was lurking inside all along," Hannah said with a laugh.

Jolyn couldn't help smiling.

"It's unbelievable that a sweet kid like Mandy sprang from that she-devil. Guess she takes after her father."

Her smile died at the reminder of Mandy's questionable parentage, which maybe wasn't so questionable, depending on a person's point of view.

"She must," Jolyn said, giving a safe response.

"For the record, I'm happy you and Chase are together."

"We're not together," Jolyn answered quickly.

"Really?" Hannah's frown didn't disguise the twinkle in her eyes. "So, you left your truck here all last night for another reason?"

"I…um…" Jolyn should have been better prepared and concocted a reply for the inevitable questions. "I came by early this morning to fix a…bad breaker."

"That's your story and you're sticking to it, huh?"

"Until I come up with a better one," she said lamely.

Hannah howled with laughter.

Jolyn noticed Chase's Aunt Susan casting them stern glances. Great. Chase's whole family must know and probably disapproved of her. She'd been so busy worrying about repercussions with her family, she'd forgotten to consider his.

"Don't mind my mom," Hannah said.

"It's hard not to."

"There's no love lost between her and SherryAnne."

"None between your mom and me, either."

"You're wrong." Hannah set her empty punch cup on a wrought-iron patio table. "She wants to see Chase happy. If you're what makes him happy, she'll support you one hundred percent."

"Hmm." Jolyn scrunched her mouth to one side.

"Okay. Eighty percent. But she'll come around eventually. Especially with me at your back."

"Why would you do that?" Jolyn asked.

"Simple. You and Chase were friends before you were lovers."

She tried not to cringe at Hannah's casual use of the term *lovers*.

"I think being friends is really important." Hannah gestured expansively. "There's always that magic at first. He's wonderful. You're walking around on cloud nine. Blah, blah, blah. But then the magic ends and then what's left? If you have a strong friendship, a lot."

"When did you get so wise?" Jolyn asked in amazement. She still thought of Hannah as a kid.

"College," Hannah said with a wink.

Jolyn sighed deeply. With Hannah rooting for her, maybe she and Chase really did have a shot at it

"I know we're not buddies or anything, not yet," Hannah went on. "But I'm going to give you some advice."

"I like what you've said so far."

"Cool." Hannah grinned. "Well, here goes. Don't let SherryAnne run you off, and believe me, she'll try. Not because she wants Chase so much as because she doesn't want you to have him."

"I figured that out already."

"I'm serious, Jolyn. If you hadn't split the last time, things might have turned out differently."

"I'm not sure about that."

"I am." Hannah turned in her chair to stare straight and hard at Jolyn. "I'm not saying it'll be easy for you and Chase." She rolled her eyes. "Hell, no it won't be, not with my family. But you guys can make it. If you just stick it out and don't run scared like before."

Is that what she'd done when she'd left to join the show all those years ago? Run scared?

"Fight for him, Jolyn," Hannah said. When her mother called her over, she patted Jolyn's knee and jumped up. "Gotta go. Nice talking to you."

Jolyn watched Mandy and her friends play a game of Ping-Pong but she didn't really see them. She was too busy mulling over what Hannah had said and seeing the past in a brand-new light.

CHASE STOOD AT the window watching heat lightning paint spiderwebs in a starless night sky and thinking how the impending storm perfectly mirrored his mood. Dark. Grim. Edgy.

The summer had been an especially dry one and many would be grateful for the rain. Chase wasn't ungrateful. He just wished the downpour would hold off until tomorrow.

SherryAnne had used the excuse of the storm to delay returning to the inn after Mandy's party. She was even now in Mandy's room, tucking her in bed and reading her a story like she was four rather than nine. Mandy didn't mind. She relished the attention her mother was paying her.

It was Chase, however, who'd have to deal with the brokenhearted little girl SherryAnne left behind when she went away again.

Barrel racing was a tough sport. Not that SherryAnne wasn't good, but she was considerably older than most of the riders she competed against. Were she smart, she'd retire before she got hurt.

He halfway hoped she'd meet another man and get remarried. A man who lived in Texas or Wyoming or any of the dozen other states her travels took her to. Anywhere but Blue Ridge. He did wish she'd visit Mandy more often, though. Four or five times a year instead of once.

Chase raked a hand through his hair and closed his eyes. Lord, he was tired. It had been one hell of a weekend, crazy busy and filled with highs and lows. Spending the night with Jolyn had been the most incredible high, his ex-wife's visit the lowest low.

"She's finally asleep," SherryAnne said, joining him in the living room.

Chase continued staring out the window. "I can't believe she stayed up this late."

"It's only nine-thirty."

"She's been going nonstop for days."

"Honestly, Chase. She's not a child anymore."

He turned around. "So why were you reading her a story?"

She leveled a warning finger at him. "Not the same thing."

He didn't disagree, only because he was too tired to argue. "If it rains tonight, you might have to cancel that ride I heard you and Mandy talking about."

"I have to cancel it anyway."

"Oh?"

"I got a call earlier on my cell phone. I'll be leaving first thing in the morning."

"One day, SherryAnne? That's all you could spare for Mandy?"

"There's a horse I'm trying to buy in Oklahoma. The owner finally decided to put him on the market and agreed to give me first right of refusal. I have to be there by Wednesday."

"A horse?" Chase couldn't believe his ears. "You'd choose a horse over Mandy?"

"A champion horse. I can win on him, Chase." Her eyes flashed with an excitement he hadn't seen once all day, not even when she hugged their daughter after a year-long absence.

"Will you at least come for breakfast and say goodbye?"

"I don't know." She had the decency to look chagrined. "I have to be on the road pretty early."

"Then I guess I'll see you next year," he said dismissively.

"Actually, there's something I need to discuss with you."

Her tone was sweet. Honey on the comb. With Sherry-Anne, that meant only one thing. She wanted something from him.

"What's that?"

She let the ax fall. "My spousal maintenance."

"I won't give you an increase." He was already paying her too much, one of the conditions of getting full custody of Mandy. Another two years and his obligation was fulfilled.

"I'm not asking for an increase."

"No?"

She clasped her hands together in front of her and took a deep breath. "I need an advance."

"How much?"

"All of it."

"You're joking," he said flatly.

"I'm not."

"Forget it."

"Chase, please. Listen to me before you say no."

"I don't have that kind of money."

"Of course you do. You just built a new clinic and hired an assistant."

"Not that it's any of your business, but I refinanced the house. My new monthly payment is half again what the old one was."

"So, take out a second mortgage."

"I'm not giving you an advance."

"I've got to buy that horse."

"Barrel-racing horses cost a small fortune. Two years of your spousal maintenance won't come close."

"It would be enough for a down payment. And if you co-signed the note—"

"You're out of your mind."

"I only have a few more years left to compete." Her voice dropped, grew harsher. "I can't win a championship without a decent horse. This one will take me to the national finals."

"Find someone else to finance your lifestyle," he said bitterly. "One of your boyfriends." SherryAnne seldom lacked for male companionship.

Her lips thinned to a very straight, very narrow line.

"No takers? You must be losing your charm."

"Shut up, you bastard."

He'd obviously struck a nerve. Barrel racing wasn't the only competitive event in the rodeo world.

"Give me the money, Chase. Cosign the loan."

"I told you no." He turned and walked toward the kitchen.

She cut in front of him. "Give me the money or I swear, Chase, I'll tell Mandy you might not be her father."

Anger rose up inside him. At SherryAnne and at himself for not making her sign an agreement when they'd divorced. The oversight had come back to haunt him more than once.

"You wouldn't dare." He spoke low.

She shouted. "Try me!"

Apprehension replaced anger. What if she really did tell Mandy? She'd threatened Chase before, though not as vehemently. Studying her, he decided she might make good this time. SherryAnne was desperate, and desperate people behaved irrationally.

He stood his ground, refusing to let her see how much she unnerved him. One hint of weakness and SherryAnne would go in for the kill.

"I should have known better. You didn't come here to spend Mandy's birthday with her. You came for money. That's so like you."

"Save the guilt trip for another visit." She sneered at him. "I'm in a hurry."

"I can't give you money I don't have."

"Find it. Borrow it. I don't care."

"Even if I did agree, I couldn't raise the money in two days. It took me months to refinance the house."

"Not my problem."

She had to be bluffing. And maybe what he needed to do was call her on it.

"You want a change in our spousal agreement, hire an attorney and take me to court."

Hands on hips, she stepped forward and put her face right up in his. "I swear, Chase, I'll tell Mandy your new girlfriend's brother could be her real dad."

He didn't so much as blink. "You'd actually walk into her bedroom, wake her up and tell her something like that? It's not me or Jolyn she'll hate, SherryAnne. It's you."

Her chin drooped, but only for a moment. Then she was her old self once more. "Do you honestly think Mandy will want to live with you after that?"

Inside, Chase shook. He'd be damned if he let SherryAnne see it. "Do you honestly think she'd live with *you?*"

She shot him a look of pure hatred. "I'll call you in the morning. You can tell me where and how I can pick up the money."

This time, her demand lacked force.

"I'll tell Mandy goodbye for you." Chase was never so glad to see the door shut behind her.

With unsteady hands, he picked up the phone and dialed Jolyn's cell number. It was almost ten. Given the early morning hours she kept, chances were good she'd already gone to bed. But he needed to talk to her. Badly. She was his lover. More than that, she was his friend.

"Hello." She answered quickly enough to assure him he hadn't awakened her.

"It's me."

"Are you okay?"

He must sound bad if she could tell something was wrong in one short sentence. "No, I'm not. SherryAnne and I just had a really bad fight."

"Oh, Chase. And on Mandy's birthday."

"Yeah." Outside, thunder rumbled. Not a night for driving. He asked anyway. "Is there any chance you can come over?"

She paused for only a second. "I'll be right there."

Chapter Sixteen

Chase and Jolyn sat in lawn chairs on his back porch, drinking leftover punch from the party and waiting for the storm to break. The temperature had dropped only five degrees since the afternoon, and the air was heavy with humidity.

"SherryAnne can't be serious," Jolyn said.

"That's what I keep telling myself." Chase had recounted his entire argument with SherryAnne to Jolyn. Like him, she'd been appalled at his ex-wife's selfishness. "I never thought she'd stoop to involving Mandy."

"Do you suppose the horse is only an excuse?"

"For what?"

"Maybe she needs the money for another reason, and she's too embarrassed to say."

"You always come to her defense. Even when she doesn't deserve it." Once, he'd admired her devotion. Now, it irked him.

"I don't always come to her defense." Hurt showed on Jolyn's face, rang in her voice.

"Sorry. I shouldn't have said that." Chase felt like a heel. She didn't deserve to be a target for his frustration.

"Forget it." Jolyn shrugged off his apology. "Sounds like she put you through the wringer tonight."

"What makes you think there's another reason besides the horse?" he asked in a more conversational tone.

"Nothing, really. I just don't understand SherryAnne anymore. Abandoning her daughter in order to be a competitive barrel racer is one thing. Vowing to tell Mandy you might not…about Steven…is just despicable."

Chase stared at the darkness beyond the porch. Not four hours earlier they'd sat in these same chairs, surrounded by friends and family. So much had changed in such a short span of time it hardly seemed like the same day.

"I'll just have to keep SherryAnne away from Mandy."

"Mandy won't understand why."

"I can't take the chance. SherryAnne might let something slip."

"Can I ask something without you getting mad?"

"Uh-oh." He grimaced but good naturedly.

"Have you ever considered having the DNA testing done?"

"What!" Of all the things he'd thought she might ask, this was the last.

"Discretely, of course. You wouldn't have to tell anyone until the results came back."

An ice-cold ball of fear settled in his stomach. "DNA testing won't solve my problems," he said stonily.

"But it would. Really." Jolyn appeared to be unaware of the turmoil building inside him. "When the results came back positive, SherryAnne and my mother would have nothing to hold over your head."

"And if the results came back negative?" Here was the crux of the matter and what scared Chase the most. "What then?"

"You and Mandy would go on like before," she said, as if it were just that simple.

Only it wouldn't be like before and it certainly wouldn't be simple.

He'd know he wasn't Mandy's real father, and that wasn't something he could live with.

"No."

"This could fix everything," she insisted.

"Or destroy everything."

"Mandy's your daughter. I believe it. Steven believes it."

"You've been talking to him about my problems?"

"Not about the DNA testing. Mandy, yes. A couple of weeks ago."

"I see," he said evenly.

"No one would be more relieved to learn Mandy was your daughter than him."

"*I'd* be more relieved."

"Yes—you, of course."

"I'd rather you didn't discuss me with your brother," he grumbled. "If you don't mind."

"All right."

Her tone rankled him. "I mean it."

"And I won't," she said with a touch of impatience, then sighed. "At least consider having the test done."

"Why are you suddenly pressuring me?"

"I'm not."

"That's what it feels like." Chase had always counted on Jolyn's support. Had she shifted that support to Dottie? "Your mother's sick," he said abruptly.

"Yes. What are you getting at?"

He sensed her eyes on him but didn't return her gaze. "That you'd like me to have the DNA testing done so your sick mother will have proof she's Mandy's grandmother."

Her stare intensified. "Did last night mean anything to you?"

"Of course it did."

"Look at me when you say that."

He turned his head, met her eyes. "Last night meant more to me than I ever thought possible."

"For me, too," she said, as if that should clear the air.

Only it didn't. "Then why suggest I have the DNA testing?"

"Because I thought the positive results would finally free you, all of us, from this damn dark cloud we've been living under for years. Is that so horrible?"

"I will not lose my daughter. I'm sorry your mother's sick, but Mandy's my entire life."

"And what about me? What am I to you? Lover? Girlfriend? One-night stand?"

"I thought you were my friend."

"I am. Even when you haven't treated me like one."

"What are you talking about?"

"The night of our senior dance. You took me home and kissed me. You led me to believe you and SherryAnne were finished and that we, we…" She paused. "That we had something special."

"We did," he said softly.

"Then how come you blew me off later?"

She stood so abruptly, the plastic lawn chair wobbled and nearly tipped over. Chase reached out and steadied it. She glared at him, then swung around as if to leave through the kitchen door.

"Wait," he snapped. "Don't go."

To his relief, she stopped. She didn't, however, return to her chair.

"You're right," he said. "I treated you badly. And there's no excuse for it other than I was young and stupid and thinking with a part of my body not my brain. But that was a long time ago. And in the grand scheme of things, pretty insignificant compared to Mandy and the very real possibility SherryAnne will ruin my relationship with her."

Several seconds of silence passed before Jolyn spoke.

"Yes, my mother is sick," she said without emotion. "Maybe very sick. But I assure you, Chase, I didn't suggest you have the DNA testing for her sake. Only yours."

"Are you sure?"

She went rigid. "This conversation is over."

"Jolyn."

When she headed for the door, he didn't stop her. A moment later, he was alone on the porch. He spent the next fifteen minutes watching the storm gain momentum and trying to convince himself he had no reason to feel guilty as hell.

EVENTUALLY, CHASE dragged himself into the house. He regretted his fight with Jolyn but was convinced he was right. Dottie factored into her argument that he have the DNA testing done, whether she realized it or not.

Something told him sleep wouldn't come easy tonight. He'd crawl between the sheets only to remember Jolyn and the hours they'd lain together last night, making love.

"Shit," he muttered to himself.

He should call her in the morning, see how she was doing. No, wait. Her mother was having outpatient surgery. The reminder cemented Chase's resolve to stay strong. No one was going to coerce him into having the test. And if that decision cost him his relationship with Jolyn, so be it.

Was that what he wanted?

"No," he answered out loud, hating that it might be his only choice.

He went down the hall to Mandy's room. It was his nightly habit to check on her before he went to bed even though she'd passed the age where she needed checking on.

Pushing open the door to her room, Chase peeked inside. An unexpected rush of air struck him in the face. Strange. Mandy didn't like to sleep with the window open, especially during a storm. In the darkness, he heard Lickety whining.

"Quiet, girl," he whispered and crossed the room silently. The window was wide open. Lickety stood on the floor beneath it, her nose raised in the air. Chase started to close the window, then realized the screen was missing.

"What the—" A chill ran through his body. He reached for the light on Mandy's bedside table and switched it on.

Her bed was empty.

"Mandy!" he called in a panic.

She didn't answer.

A terror unequal to anything Chase had ever experienced seized him.

Where in God's name had she gone?

Stopping only long enough to grab a flashlight from the kitchen drawer, he bolted through the back door. He had no idea where to start looking for Mandy, only that he had to.

Lickety ran toward the barn. Chase followed, also running, his feet slipping on the uneven ground. Inside the barn, he stopped to turn on a light.

The startled horses, already nervous because of the thunder and lightning, tossed their heads and whinnied. Matilda reared and kicked the side panel of her stall. Lickety tore up the aisle and then back down, her nose glued to the ground.

Chase walked more slowly, carefully scanning his surroundings, hoping that Mandy was hiding somewhere in the barn. She must have heard him and SherryAnne fighting. Why else would she run away? They'd forgotten to lower their voices. Hell, they'd been loud enough for the neighbors to hear every word.

Dammit! Could he have been more stupid? If she heard… That meant she knew he might not be her father. What must she be thinking and feeling?

He had to find her. He must. And somehow, some way, he'd make everything right again.

"Easy now."

Settling the horses as he walked down the aisle, he peered into each stall and swept the back corners with the flashlight. He didn't expect to find Mandy. More likely, she was hiding in the tack room or the garage. Still, he checked each stall, even the empty ones, just to be sure.

When he came to the end, his heart nearly stopped beating.

Mandy's little horse, Cinnamon, was gone.

He ran back down the aisle to the tack room. Shoving open the door, he turned on the light.

Cinnamon's saddle was missing, as was her bridle.

A low groan of despair escaped Chase. In the next second, rain started falling. Fat drops hit the metal barn roof like a shower of bullets.

Chase raced back to the house. By the time he reached the back porch, the rain was coming down in buckets.

Terror gripped him, paralyzed him, tore him in two. His daughter was missing. She'd run away from home. And the rainstorm to beat all rainstorms had just begun.

JOLYN PACED the empty house, listening to the thunder unleash its fury.

She'd held back her tears after her fight with Chase until she'd reached her truck, then cried all the way home, telling herself she was a fool for believing they had a future together.

Once home, she replayed their argument, and after some thoughtful introspection, changed her mind. Chase had been right. Her suggestion that he have the DNA testing was, to some degree, motivated by her mother's health. And Jolyn's own best interests.

If Chase proved to be Mandy's father, Jolyn's mother and SherryAnne would lose their hold over him. Her brother would also be out from under SherryAnne's thumb.

But what if the results were negative? How could she suggest Chase live with the knowledge that he wasn't Mandy's father and expect him to believe she cared for him?

For the fourth time in the last hour, Jolyn started up the stairs for her bedroom only to stop and return to the den. She knew she wouldn't be able to sleep, and tossing and turning would just frustrate her further.

Yet, she needed sleep in order to get through the day ahead, and 5:30 a.m. was just six short hours away. After checking on the Buchanans' solarium job and meeting the painters at her office, she would leave for the hospital.

Assuming all went well with her mother's surgery, she'd be back on the road to Blue Ridge by midafternoon. Her father would bring her mother home that evening. Kenny Jr. had agreed to cover the post office for as long as necessary. Jolyn fervently wished the arrangements they'd made were temporary and that life quickly returned to normal.

She jumped when the phone rang suddenly. Who could be calling at this late hour?

"Hello?" she said into the phone.

"Jolyn?"

"Chase?" Her startled heart began to beat wildly.

"Sorry to disturb you."

"It's all right. I was still up." She contemplated what to say to him.

"I know this is going to sound strange, but you haven't by chance heard from or seen Mandy tonight?"

"Mandy? No."

Chase swore under his breath. "You were my last hope."

She heard the desperation in his voice. "Is something wrong?"

"Mandy ran away."

"What?"

"She took off on Cinnamon. Between nine and ten, I'm guessing."

"She's riding?" His announcement shocked Jolyn to her very core. "In this storm?"

"Yeah. I'm afraid so." His voice caught.

"Oh, no. What happened?"

"I think she must have overheard SherryAnne and I arguing."

"Oh, Chase. You don't think she heard us, too?" Jolyn couldn't bear to think she'd played a part in Mandy's disappearance.

"I doubt it. If anything, she probably snuck out while we were talking. She went out the window and could have easily cut around and through the pasture to the barn."

And they'd been too busy disagreeing to notice anything, Jolyn thought miserably. "What can I do to help?"

"Nothing. Just call if you hear from her."

"I will, I promise. What are you going to do?"

"I've phoned all her friends that I can think of and SherryAnne at the inn."

"How's she taking it?"

"She's upset. And feels responsible. She wants to help with the search tomorrow. I told her she should stay in town in case Mandy shows up."

"What search?"

"I contacted my commander in the sheriff's posse. I didn't know what else to do."

She remembered that Chase belonged to the mounted search and rescue. "I think that's smart. No sense taking any chances." If Mandy went into the nearby mountains during a thunderstorm… Jolyn shuddered.

"We can't start the search until daybreak. Everyone's meeting in the center of town in front of the library. We'll split up into teams to cover more territory."

"I'll be there."

"I can't ask that of you."

"You're not asking, I'm volunteering."

"But your mother's surgery is tomorrow."

"Dad and Steven will be with her. And they'll understand if I'm not." Tears pricked her eyes. "Chase, you've got to find her. She can't be out in this weather for long."

"No, she can't," he said in a hoarse whisper.

"I'll come over if you like."

"Thanks. But I've got a lot to do to get ready for the morning. And I'm still contacting people."

"If you need anything, *anything,*" she reiterated, "call. I don't care what time it is." She doubted she'd sleep even one wink tonight.

There was a brief silence on the line. "After what I said to you earlier tonight, I wouldn't blame you if—"

"Stop it," she interrupted. "It really doesn't matter who's at fault. Finding Mandy is all that matters." She breathed deeply. "You're going to get her back, Chase. She couldn't have gone far, not on Cinnamon."

"I hope you're right."

"I'll see you in the morning," she said, wishing she had more than words to comfort him.

Chapter Seventeen

Chase spent most of the night driving around town in the rain, searching for Mandy and grimacing at every crack of thunder and streak of lightning. Around 4:30 a.m. he headed out to the barn to saddle Matilda and gather equipment.

This was all his fault. If he hadn't argued with SherryAnne, or had at least shown the good sense to take their argument out of Mandy's earshot, his daughter wouldn't have run away. If anything happened to her, he'd never forgive himself.

Climbing onto Matilda, he galloped down the road. The library came into view just as the eastern horizon went from pitch-black to an overcast predawn gray. It had stopped raining about two or three hours ago but the air had a damp feel to it. The weather report on the twenty-four-hour news station predicted more rain.

Chase hated to think of Mandy spending the night outside, possibly in the nearby hills and woods. His one consolation was that while wet, it wasn't cold. She might be uncomfortable depending on where she'd found refuge, but she'd survive the elements. And the two of them had ridden the area enough that she knew her way around.

He felt a tightness in his chest as he came upon the library. Even in the dim light of a gloomy dawn, he could make out a huge number of vehicles and riders, see the zigzagging beams of a dozen lanterns and flashlights. Twenty-five people, at least, had shown up to help in the search for Mandy and more were coming every minute. Surely with so many of them looking, they would find her, and quickly.

Jolyn was there—he saw her right away. She stood by Mike's truck, sipping a cup of coffee. Chase's aunt and uncle had also arrived, along with the entire Blue Ridge volunteer fire department and many of the mounted posse members. Gage was there, too, with Aubrey. Chase hoped that Mandy wouldn't need the services of a nurse.

He dismounted and was met by Mrs. Cutter. She was passing out coffee and donuts. Chase accepted a coffee but declined the donut. He couldn't bring himself to eat until they found Mandy.

Tying Matilda to one of the horse trailers, he went to find Chuck, his platoon leader.

"Thanks for coming," he repeated over and over, shaking hands and accepting well wishes as he made his way toward the mounted posse members.

"We're going to find her." Uncle Joseph clapped Chase on the back. "Don't worry."

"Oh, sweetie." Aunt Susan pulled him into a tearful embrace. "How are you holding up?"

Conversation was difficult for Chase, so he said little.

SherryAnne arrived then, having walked over from the inn. It was obvious most people weren't aware she was in town. They greeted her with surprise, but also concern, extending their well wishes to her as they had to Chase.

Sobbing, she threw herself at him. "Chase! What are we going to do?"

He initially resisted, then lightly patted her shoulder. SherryAnne's distress was genuine. And if they were going to find Mandy, they needed to work together, not bicker or blame each other for what had happened.

"You stay here," he told her and explained how the posse

would set up a temporary command post in the community center. "We'll be in constant radio contact. Mrs. Payne is at the house in case Mandy comes home."

Rain began falling again, more of a drizzle than a downpour. Plastic ponchos and hats were pulled from packs and quickly donned. A few umbrellas snapped open, and people huddled more closely together.

Minutes later, Chuck called Chase over. A map lay open on the hood of his truck. The posse members were discussing which surrounding areas to search first, how many teams to split into and which roads or trails to take. Equipment and supplies were distributed, including radios, GPS monitors, ropes, tools, first-aid kits and water bottles.

Gage and Mike had organized a team of volunteers who were going out on ATVs and in four-wheel-drive trucks.

About that time, two vehicles from the sheriff's department arrived. Chase had called the sheriff the previous night to report Mandy missing and they'd promised to send some deputies to help with the search. Chase estimated there were now forty or fifty people assembled.

"Let's go, men," Chuck said after briefing the deputies.

Everyone went in different directions.

Chase cut through the crowd to the trailer where he'd tied Matilda. He'd be riding with Chuck in the woods and hills along the main road out of Blue Ridge.

"Chase?" Jolyn walked toward him, leading Sinbad.

"Hi."

After an awkward moment, they hugged.

"Did you get any sleep?" she asked.

"No, not really." He shifted impatiently, anxious to get started on the search. The rain was falling heavier by the minute. "I have to go."

"I don't mean to keep you, but I just had an idea where Mandy might be."

"Where?"

"The old Ladderback mine. Remember, I took her and Elizabeth there that one day we were riding and you got called away on a search."

"Why would she go there?"

"It's just a hunch, really. But I showed her the initials you'd carved in the beams. Yours and SherryAnne's. She seemed fascinated by them."

"You may be right. She's asked me twice since then to take her back to the mine. Will you ride with me?"

"Sure."

"Let me go tell Chuck."

JOLYN RODE WITH Chase and two other members of the Mounted Posse only until they reached the part of the trail where it split. The posse members took the trail leading to Neglian Creek crossing. Jolyn and Chase headed up the much steeper slope to the old Ladderback mine.

Fortunately, the thunder and lightning had stopped during the night. But a strong wind whipped through the trees, causing the rain to strike them in the face and hamper visibility.

Halfway up the mountainside Sinbad began breathing hard, but the younger, endurance-trained Matilda climbed the slope like an army tank. Both horses frequently slipped and slid, their hooves struggling to find solid purchase on the wet rocks and muddy ground.

"Good boy," Jolyn murmured and patted Sinbad's neck.

Had she been alone, she would have stopped for a short rest. Chase, who rode in front of her, didn't appear to notice Sinbad's labored breathing or was too focused on finding Mandy for anything else to penetrate.

Jolyn pulled back on the reins, thinking she'd tell Chase to go on without her and that she'd follow after a short rest.

Sinbad would have none of it. He fought the reins, dropping his head and forging onward. He might be getting older but his pride was intact.

"Okay, buddy. Your call." She let up on the reins and used the back of her hand to wipe the worst of the rain from her face.

Trees grew closer together the higher they rode. Cedars gave way to majestic pines and tall oaks. Bushes were thick with summer leaves. Jolyn and Chase stayed to the ever-narrowing, ever-steepening trail.

"Look!" Chase pointed to a metal post sticking out of the ground. The mine lay about a hundred and fifty feet ahead.

Jolyn's anxiety increased. Would they find Mandy or had she led them on a wild-goose chase?

Beside the trail, the once-trickling stream rushed down the mountain, carrying leaves, small branches and other natural debris. Fed by runoff from the rain, it had grown to four times its normal size. Both horses eyed the stream nervously and stayed to the far side of the trail.

When they reached the foot of the rise leading to the mine, Chase stopped. "Listen," he said.

Jolyn did…and heard it, too! The distant sound of another horse whinnying.

Chase pushed Matilda hard up the rise. In another minute, horse and rider disappeared from sight.

Sinbad was slower to respond, but he did as he was asked, proving his worth and devotion once again.

Blood pounding, heart hammering, Jolyn crested the rise. The first thing she saw was Chase. He'd dismounted and was standing at the side of the raging stream. Across the stream and twenty or so feet above them, Cinnamon stood outside the mine entrance, tied to the branch of a pine tree. She tossed her head and whinnied again to her barn mate.

"Oh, thank God," Jolyn said. Weak with relief, she let her head fall momentarily into her hand.

"Mandy." Chase cupped his hands to his mouth and hollered louder. "Mandy! Where are you?"

Jolyn was beginning to fear that something dreadful had occurred when a small head appeared at the entrance to the mine.

"Daddy?"

"Mandy!" Chase called in a choked voice, then braced his hands on his knees and closed his eyes.

Jolyn, too, was overcome with emotion. Her tears of joy mingled with the rain.

"Are you all right?" Chase hollered a few seconds later.

"Yes." She sounded both scared and relieved. "Are you mad at me?"

"No, honey. I'm not mad. I'm too glad to see you to be mad." He pulled his radio from the clip on his belt.

"I wanted to come home this morning but I was afraid to cross the stream." Stepping out of the mine opening, she walked to where the ledge dropped off, hugging her thin frame. She wore a T-shirt and pants, but no jacket or poncho.

"You stay there, honey," Chase said. "Don't move. I'm coming across to get you." He turned to Jolyn and in a softer voice, said, "Thank you."

"I'm so glad we found her."

"Me, too."

Chase nodded, and Jolyn felt a small spark of the connection they'd formed the night they'd made love.

After radioing in their location, Chase mounted Matilda and swung her around. "You wait here," he said over his shoulder to Jolyn, then drove his heels into Matilda's sides.

The mare took two steps toward the stream, then came to an abrupt stop. Dropping her head almost to the ground, she snorted and pawed the loose, wet dirt.

"Come on!" Chase jerked her head up and tried again to get her to cross. She refused, this time spinning on her hind hooves and dancing away from the stream, her eyes wide with fright. "Damn horse." He looked at Jolyn, his features strained with annoyance. "She hates crossing water."

"Can I help?"

"Get behind me. See if you can't push her into jumping."

Jolyn did as Chase instructed. Still, the mare refused, bucking and kicking at Sinbad and nearly unseating Chase.

"Forget it," he snarled. "I'll go upstream. See if there's a narrower place I can cross by foot. You wait here, keep an eye on Mandy."

"Okay." Jolyn nodded.

"Daddy, where are you going?" Mandy hollered and started down the steep path leading from the mine.

"Stay there," Chase ordered sternly. "I'm coming."

Mandy let out a shriek.

Jolyn's head snapped around.

Mandy teetered precariously on the ledge, which appeared to shift and move beneath her feet. With a sickening crunch, a large chunk of earth gave way, broke off and slid down the mountainside, carrying her with it.

As if in slow motion, her legs went out from under her. She pitched forward, hit the moving mass of earth face-first and rolled. Her screams were drowned out by the rain and the roar of the landslide.

"Mandy!" Chase hollered, coming up out of the saddle.

Jolyn tugged Sinbad's head to the right and urged him into a fast trot. They followed Mandy, momentum sending the little girl head over heels down the slope at a horrifying rate. Jolyn couldn't remember ever feeling so scared or so helpless.

Twenty feet down the mountainside, Mandy veered off the path and toppled over another, steeper, ledge. By some small miracle she rolled between several trees…only to come to a sudden and bone-crunching stop when she plowed straight into a large boulder.

She lay very, very still.

Jolyn hopped off Sinbad, dropped her reins and put a foot in the stream. The strong current nearly sucked her boot off.

"Wait," Chase yelled. He was running Matilda straight at her.

All at once he steered Matilda away from the stream. Spinning her around, he charged the raging water at break-neck speed. For one split second, it looked as if Matilda would do as her rider commanded and jump.

Chase wasn't prepared for her abrupt halt two feet from the bank. He sailed over the mare's head and landed with a splash in the water.

Jolyn ran toward him. "Chase!"

He surfaced seconds later, sodden but apparently all right. He had trouble maintaining his footing as the current dragged at him and threatened to pull him under.

"I'll get a rope," Jolyn called and raced for Matilda. The horse remained in the same place, her long legs trembling, her nostrils flaring.

"No. I'm fine. Get Mandy."

"Chase."

"Get her!"

Jolyn ran back to Sinbad and swung onto his back…then just stood there.

How to reach Mandy? The water was too treacherous to risk. Riding either up or down the mountainside looking for a narrower crossing would take too long. Mandy still hadn't moved and could be seriously injured.

Jolyn had no choice.

With sweat-dampened palms, she gripped the reins and backed Sinbad up before she lost her courage. Ten feet. Twenty feet. Thirty feet. Aiming him in the direction of the stream, she patted his neck and whispered into his twitching ears, "Please. For me. One last jump."

He gave it to her.

Hooves thundering, legs extending, Sinbad charged the

stream. At the same instant his front feet left the ground, Jolyn hovered low on his neck. They sailed over the water, wind whipping them, rain pelting them, and hung suspended in midair for one agonizing second before he hit the ground on the opposite bank with enough force to jar her brain.

Jolyn nearly fell, but managed to right herself at the last instant. Sinbad slid, his feet flying out from under him. All at once, he found his footing, and the world stopped spinning out of control. He seemed to know where to take Jolyn without being asked. A minute later they reached Mandy. She lay pressed up against the boulder amid a pile of mud, leaves, small branches and rocks, her limbs twisted at odd angles. Jolyn hurriedly dismounted and knelt by her side.

Mandy's pale skin stood out like chalk beneath the brown streaks and smudges covering her face. She didn't move even when Jolyn spoke to her. No eyelid fluttered, no pinkie twitched.

Jolyn's insides clenched and, for a moment, she imagined the unimaginable. She raised her hand only to hesitate, afraid to touch Mandy, afraid of the cold and stillness her fingers might encounter.

All at once she saw it. The shallow rise and fall of Mandy's chest. Jolyn touched Mandy's face and was rewarded with the tiniest of moans.

Thank you, thank you!

She looked for Chase. He'd crawled out of the water and onto her side of the stream. Drenched from head to toe, he struggled to a standing position.

"She's alive," Jolyn yelled to him because it was what he'd want to know first. What he *needed* to know.

"How badly is she hurt?" he hollered back.

"It looks bad. She's not moving."

Chase ran down the slope toward them, careless of his own safety. Jolyn worried he, too, might fall. As soon as he reached them, he dropped to the ground beside Mandy. Laying a hand on her face, he tenderly brushed the hair from her eyes.

Some basic first-aid training learned over the years popped into Jolyn's head. "I don't think we should move her."

"I lost my radio in the stream," he said. "Will you ride for help?"

Jolyn rose and immediately caught sight of two riders at the base of the mountain, their yellow rain ponchos visible through the trees. She thought they might be the same two men she and Chase had ridden with earlier.

"Someone's coming," she told Chase and waved wildly. "Hey! Up here."

They waved back.

"Tell them we need a medical helicopter," Chase said, his complexion as pale as his daughter's.

"Mandy's injured," she called to the men. "We need a helicopter."

"We're on it," one of the men called back.

Jolyn knelt beside Chase and placed a hand on his arm. His poncho had come off, and his shirt was soaked. "Are you cold?"

He shook his head. His eyes, so full of worry and desperation, never left Mandy. "She can't die."

"She won't."

"I don't know what I'll do if I lose her." Emotion made his voice husky and uneven.

Jolyn swallowed before speaking, afraid her own voice might crack. She must be strong at all costs. For Chase. Just in case…

"Mandy's going to make it," she said determinedly.

"I love her so much." He stroked Mandy's cheek with his fingertips. Gently. Heart-wrenchingly. "She's my daughter. She's always been my daughter."

Jolyn quit fighting her tears. She'd been wrong to suggest

he have the DNA testing. No one had the right to do that no matter how noble the reason.

And if she hadn't been so stupid, if she hadn't put her own wants and wishes ahead of Chase's and Mandy's, she might have one day become a member of Chase's beautiful and loving family.

She prayed with all her heart that it wasn't too late.

"How is she?" one of the riders called. They'd scaled the slope and were approaching the trees. In another second, they broke through and waited on the opposite side of the stream.

"She's still unconscious," Jolyn answered.

Chase didn't look up. He'd taken one of Mandy's hands in his and was squeezing her fingers.

"Helicopter should be here shortly," the man said.

It was the longest, most grueling twenty minutes Jolyn had ever spent and must have felt like a lifetime to Chase. The whir of distant propellers was a welcome relief.

Mandy had stirred once or twice during their wait but that was all. Jolyn thought the injured girl might have grown paler and colder to the touch. It might also have been her own nerves getting the best of her.

One of the men had radioed in and they were able to speak to Chase's cousin-in-law, Aubrey. She'd advised them that Mandy had probably gone into shock and to take precautions. Disturbing her as little as possible, they'd covered her with Jolyn's poncho to keep her warm.

The helicopter flew over the stream and landed in a clearing at the base of the mountain. Two uniformed figures jumped to the ground. One of them carried a medical case, the other a portable stretcher. They came at a dead run.

Time seemed to speed up after that.

Jolyn stood back, watching as the EMTs took Mandy's vitals, conducted a quick examination, hooked her up to an IV, stabilized her neck and loaded her onto the stretcher. All within a few minutes. They were in constant radio contact with a doctor, who advised them what to do.

"All set." At the signal, the EMTs lifted Mandy and started carrying her down the mountain to the waiting helicopter.

Chase walked beside Mandy, still holding on to her hand. Jolyn followed, leading Sinbad. The posse members had led Matilda down the mountain earlier and were waiting several hundred feet up the road. Their horses stared at the helicopter in fear and distrust. Only their riders' firm grip on the reins kept them from galloping off.

Finally, the rescue party reached level ground and approached the helicopter. Jolyn tied Sinbad to a tree.

There was so much she wanted to say to Chase, so many things in the last day she wished she hadn't said to him. Scant seconds remained before the EMTs finished loading Mandy, and Chase flew with them to the hospital in Pineville.

She opened her mouth to speak, but Chase interrupted her.

"Would you see to it Matilda gets home?"

"Absolutely. Anything else?"

"No." He squeezed her arm. "Thank you again for finding Mandy. If we hadn't been there when that ledge gave way..." He stopped, composed himself.

"We were there."

He nodded, unable to answer her.

She reached a tentative hand to him and when he opened his arms, she threw herself into his embrace. "I love you," she whispered, doubting Chase heard her over the roar of the helicopter's engine.

"We have to go," one of the EMTs shouted.

Chase extracted himself from Jolyn's hold and, with the EMTs' help, crawled through the helicopter's small opening. The pilot motioned Jolyn away.

She stepped out of range of the whirling blades. Wind blasted her, nearly knocking her off balance. Shielding her face against flying debris with her forearm, she stared as the helicopter ascended. For a brief instant, Chase appeared in a window.

Jolyn raced up the road to meet the waiting men. She was in a hurry to get to Pineville. Everything that mattered to her was waiting there—her family, the man she wanted to build her future with and a little girl who'd found a big place in Jolyn's heart.

Chapter Eighteen

Jolyn arrived at Pineville General Hospital and went straight to outpatient services, where she met her father and brother. She'd learned through several phone calls to Chase's relatives that Mandy was in surgery and nothing specific was known yet about her condition. She longed to be with him but also wanted to check on her mother. She'd decided to stay a few minutes with her family and then find Chase outside the O.R.

"How's Mom?" she asked after hugging her father and brother.

"She's in recovery," her father said. "The doctor came out a little while ago and told us everything went well."

"What did he find?"

"Don't know. He's going to talk to all four of us as soon as your mother's more alert."

"What about Mandy?" It was Steven who asked the question. "Did they find her yet?"

"Yes. A couple of hours ago. She's here now."

"At the hospital?"

"She's having surgery."

"Oh, jeez. For what?"

Jolyn filled them in, her agitation increasing with each passing minute. "I'd like to go sit with Chase if you think

Mom's going to be okay. He's got to be a wreck. You can have me paged when the doctor's ready to talk to us."

At that moment a nurse called their name. She motioned for them to accompany her to the recovery area. Jolyn's mother lay in a hospital bed, tubes and wires still attached to her and looking very much out of it, though she did greet them with a weak smile.

"How are you doing, sweetheart?" Jolyn's father bent and kissed her mother on the forehead.

"I've felt better."

Dottie's doctor stepped around the privacy curtain. "Good. You're all here." He closed the curtain behind him.

Jolyn's father sat in the only chair, his hand resting protectively atop her mother's.

"We'll start with the bad news first," the doctor said, "and then get to the good news. And that, people, is what I want you to focus on." He looked at each of them before continuing. "The lumps definitely aren't cysts."

"Do I have cancer?" Dottie asked in a scratchy voice.

"We won't know for sure until the biopsy results come back. I can tell you if you do have cancer, we've caught it early. The tumors were small. May even be benign, let's not jump to conclusions. And based on when you told me you discovered them, they were growing at a very slow rate. We removed them to be on the safe side."

"What's next?" Milt asked, his eyes red and watery.

The doctor briefly explained the various treatment courses, all of which would depend on the biopsy results. "We'll talk more at the end of the week. But again—" he patted Dottie's shoulder "—I'm optimistic. You need to be, too."

"Thank you, Doctor," Jolyn said, remembering the coin she'd tossed into the fountain at Pineville Medical Center. It looked as if her wish might just come true.

The doctor shook hands with everyone and then left. A

nurse immediately came in to take Dottie's vitals. "She can leave soon if you want to wait."

"I'd like to go see Chase," Jolyn said.

"Chase?" her mother said around the thermometer in her mouth.

"Mandy's been hurt."

"Hurt! How?"

"Dad and Steven can tell you all about it."

"We'll come find you before we leave," her father said.

"Wait." Dottie struggled to sit up.

It was Steven who paved the way for Jolyn's escape. "Let her go, Mom. She should be with Chase right now."

Jolyn hadn't told her brother about her new relationship, but the look he gave her showed that he understood and approved.

She smiled at him and said, "I'll see you in a little while."

EACH TIME ONE of the doors flew open or footsteps sounded in the hallway, Chase leaped from his seat only to sit back down, rest his elbows on his knees and stare at the floor.

What was taking so long? Mandy had been in surgery for an hour. Or was it two? He couldn't remember when exactly they'd arrived at the hospital. The helicopter ride had been a big blur.

More footsteps in the hall. He sprang to his feet again just as Jolyn entered the waiting area.

He crossed the room to her. "Thanks for coming."

"Any news?"

"Not yet." His chest constricted painfully.

He and Jolyn took a seat together. She said hello to his aunt and uncle. Both of his cousins were due to arrive shortly.

"You're here." SherryAnne stared at Jolyn, eyes narrowing when she saw how Chase gripped Jolyn's hand as if it were a lifeline.

Jolyn didn't wilt under SherryAnne's scrutiny. "I am. My mother had a procedure done this morning."

"How is she?" Chase asked.

"All right. We still have to wait for the biopsy results but the doctor sounded pretty optimistic."

"Is she sick?" Susan asked.

Jolyn apparently decided it was time to put the rumors to rest. "She found some lumps in her breasts."

"Oh, dear." Susan's expression softened. "If there's anything we can do, let us know."

"Where's that damn doctor?" SherryAnne got up and began pacing the waiting area.

Chase didn't blame her. Until Jolyn arrived, he'd felt ready to explode. But her presence had calmed his frayed nerves and eased the tension tearing him apart.

Another hour passed before the double doors burst open and the surgeon who'd operated on Mandy emerged, still wearing his scrubs. Everyone was instantly on their feet. Chase let go of Jolyn's hand and rushed to meet the surgeon. SherryAnne was right beside him.

"She's made it through, and very well under the circumstances," the surgeon said. "But she's not out of danger yet. She suffered internal injuries in the fall and was hemorrhaging severely when she arrived. We had to remove her spleen and we'll be keeping a very close watch on her kidneys, particularly her right one. She also suffered a broken collarbone and a dislocated elbow. Those injuries, however, are minor compared to her internal ones."

"Is she going to live?" SherryAnne cried.

"She's stable for the moment. The next few hours are very important. She lost a lot of blood. We had only one unit on hand to give her. There was a five-car wreck on the freeway yesterday and we used most of our supply. We put in a request with blood services for replacements. Unfortunately, the shipment won't arrive for a few hours. Possibly not until this evening."

"Can we donate blood?" Chase asked.

The surgeon frowned. "Donor blood has to be processed before it can be used." He nodded curtly. "However, we're a small hospital in a small community. And I'm not against having a backup plan when a life's on the line." His glance went from Chase to SherryAnne. "Do you know your blood type?"

"No," they said in unison.

"Not a problem. The lab can type you. I'll call down and make arrangements. One of you is bound to be compatible."

Chase didn't care who, him or SherryAnne.

"Someone will check with you shortly, let you know how your daughter's doing."

"Thank you," Chase said to the surgeon's retreating back.

"Just a minute!"

Everyone turned to see an unsteady Dottie Sutherland enter the waiting area, assisted by her husband. Steven stood behind her, and Chase felt the familiar tightening in his gut.

"What are you doing here?" Jolyn asked in surprise and alarm.

"Let Steven donate, too," Dottie said.

"No!" Jolyn took a step toward her mother.

"He could be a match for Mandy."

"Mom," Steven warned her, "this isn't your concern."

"That little girl needs blood. And she could be your daughter. My granddaughter."

"She's not."

Milt tried to propel Dottie to a chair. "You said we were just stopping by to talk to Jolyn."

"It's all right." Chase was surprised to hear his own voice. "Steven should donate, too."

"Chase." Jolyn was instantly next to him, laying a soothing hand on his arm. "You don't have to."

"I do." He smiled down at her, suddenly filled with certainty that he was doing the right thing. "What matters the most is Mandy. If she needs blood to live, I want her to have it. And I don't care who the donor is."

She stood on tiptoes and wrapped her arms around his neck, holding him tight.

He lowered his mouth and nuzzled her ear. "I heard you before."

"What's that?"

"I love you, too," he whispered.

She gasped slightly.

"Come with me to the lab. We can talk while they draw my blood."

"THEY'LL LET YOU KNOW as soon as we have the results," the lab technician said crisply.

Jolyn waited for Chase to finish up. The entire procedure of donating blood hadn't taken long, thank goodness. She knew he was anxious to get back upstairs and see if there was any word on Mandy's progress.

SherryAnne had gone last and was only just then sitting up and drinking from a juice box. Steven was also done but Jolyn suspected he was stalling until Chase left. The two of them stuck in an elevator together would make for some very cramped quarters.

The ride from the lower-level lab to the O.R. on the second floor seemed to take hours rather than a couple of minutes. Chase practically dragged Jolyn out of the elevator the instant the doors slid open.

"What's the latest?" he asked his aunt and uncle.

"Someone came by about ten minutes ago," Susan answered. "Said Mandy was holding her own."

Not worse, Jolyn thought with relief. She went over to where her parents were sitting. "Maybe you should go home, Mom. You look beat."

"I want to stay. At least until we have more news on Mandy. Steven invited us to spend another night at his house."

"Okay." Jolyn wondered if the news her mother anxiously awaited was regarding a compatible donor.

"I'm not trying to be mean," Dottie said with sincerity. "I really do love Mandy and want her to recover with all my heart."

"I'm glad to hear it," Chase answered before Jolyn could. He approached and put an arm around her shoulders. "Because Jolyn and I are getting married."

"We are?" she said in unison with everyone else in the room. SherryAnne's voice was the loudest. She and Steven had only just returned from the lab.

"As soon as Mandy's better." Chase kissed Jolyn lightly on the lips. "That is, if you're willing to make an honest man out of me."

"I am. Oh, I am." She wrapped her arms around him. "But what if—"

"Shh." He silenced her with another kiss. "Nothing is important but me, Mandy and you. The rest will fall into place."

He was right. Everything *would* fall into place. Sutherland Construction, his new clinic, her mother's health, Mandy's recovery. It would all work out perfectly. It had to.

"Mr. and Mrs. Raintree?" In all the commotion, no one had heard Mandy's surgeon come into the waiting area.

Chase and SherryAnne both spun around. "Yes?" From opposite ends of the room they converged and then bore down on him.

"I have an update on your daughter."

Everyone went utterly still.

"Her vitals are good and improving steadily." The surgeon's tone and expression remained neutral despite his heartening words. "We should be moving her into the ICU shortly. If she continues to improve I'll upgrade her condition from critical to guarded."

The room let out a collective sigh of relief.

"She's one very lucky girl," the surgeon said. "It's fortunate you found her when you did."

"Yes, it is." Chase sought out Jolyn's eyes and the look he gave her expressed his love and gratitude.

"I don't think we'll need to give Mandy another transfusion at this point," the surgeon continued. "But in a worst-case scenario, I understand one of you is a compatible donor." He consulted the clipboard he carried. "Mr. Raintree. It's you."

"No one else?" Jolyn's mother asked from her chair.

The surgeon shook his head. "Only Mr. Raintree. But I'm fairly certain we won't be needing any blood. Mandy's a fighter. I think she's going to pull through just fine."

SherryAnne broke into sobs the second the surgeon left and clung to Chase. "I'm sorry. I'm so sorry about everything. I've been a lousy mother lately."

"So change," he said, gently disengaging himself. "Mandy loves you. She'll forget the last two years."

"I was always sure you were her father." SherryAnne sniffed and wiped her nose. "I wouldn't have left her with you if I hadn't been."

"You're welcome to visit anytime, SherryAnne."

"What would you say if I quit rodeoing and moved back?"

"I'd say Mandy would be very happy."

"And what about you?"

Chase reached for Jolyn and pulled her to his side. "I'd be happy for Mandy."

"You two really are going to get married?" SherryAnne asked.

"Yes, we are," Jolyn replied, her arm around Chase's waist. "As soon as Mandy's up and about."

SherryAnne laughed and threw Jolyn for a loop by giving her a big hug. "Congratulations. To both of you."

"I hear I'm about to become a brother-in-law." Steven approached Chase and Jolyn. Rather than hugging her as she expected, he extended his hand to Chase. "I couldn't be more glad."

Chase took her brother's outstretched hand with no hesitation, and it seemed to Jolyn that the animosity between the two men was well on the way to disappearing.

"Welcome to the family," Steven said.

An O.R. nurse came through the double doors. "You can see your daughter. But only for a few minutes."

Jolyn felt Chase tense, then go slack with relief.

SherryAnne pressed her fingers to her lips and looked as if she might burst into fresh tears.

"How many can go at one time?" Chase asked.

"Two." The nurse winked broadly. "Three, if you sweet-talk me."

"SherryAnne, take Aunt Susan. I'll wait and go with Jolyn."

"You sure?"

"Hurry. Before I change my mind."

SherryAnne didn't have to be told twice. She and his aunt followed the nurse out of the waiting area.

"Chase, why didn't you go with her?" Jolyn asked when he walked over to her. "I'd have waited."

"Because Mandy can only have three visitors at a time." His gaze went to Dottie. "And I want my future mother-in-law to come with us."

"You do?" Dottie stared up at him in disbelief.

"You may not be her biological grandmother but you're going to be her stepgrandmother. Something I'm sure will delight Mandy to no end." He leaned down to give her an affectionate peck on the cheek. "And I'm hoping Jolyn's agreeable to giving you one or two more grandkids."

"Thank you, Chase." Dottie held on to him for a long moment.

Jolyn thought there might be more to her mother's gratitude than he realized, for he'd given her yet another reason to battle *and conquer* her illness.

"You're welcome," he said, shaking Milt's hand. "We're a family. In every way that counts."

He swept Jolyn up in his arms and kissed her soundly. The formerly tension-filled waiting room became a place of celebration. For Jolyn and Chase's engagement and then for Mandy when SherryAnne returned some minutes later to report that her daughter, while still drowsy, was responsive.

"You should know something before you go in there," SherryAnne said, pulling Chase aside. "Mandy asked about our argument last night."

He'd worried about exactly what and how much she heard.

"She wanted to know if what I said was true." SherryAnne's eyes welled with tears. "I told her absolutely not. That I lied because I was angry at you."

Chase was impressed that SherryAnne had taken the blame. Perhaps there was hope for her yet. "I'll talk to her, too."

"Maybe the three of us should sit down together when she's better."

"I think that's a good idea." However he had to manage it, he'd make sure Mandy knew what he'd been certain of all along. That she was *his* daughter.

Chase turned to find Jolyn standing with her mother and his heart swelled with love and hope. "Are we ready?"

He clasped their hands in his and, going slowly to accommodate his future mother-in-law, led them down the corridor to the recovery room where Mandy and their new life awaited.

Bundles of Joy—
coming next month to Superromance

Experience the romance, excitement and joy with 6 heartwarming titles.

BABY, I'M YOURS #1476 by *Carrie Weaver*

ANOTHER MAN'S BABY
(The Tulanes of Tennessee)
#1477 by *Kay Stockham*

THE MARINE'S BABY (9 Months Later)
#1478 by *Rogenna Brewer*

BE MY BABIES (Twins)
#1479 by *Kathryn Shay*

THE DIAPER DIARIES (Suddenly a Parent)
#1480 by *Abby Gaines*

HAVING JUSTIN'S BABY (A Little Secret)
#1481 by *Pamela Bauer*

Exciting, Emotional and Unexpected!

Look for these Superromance titles in March 2008.
Available wherever books are sold.

REQUEST YOUR FREE BOOKS!
2 FREE NOVELS PLUS 2
FREE GIFTS!

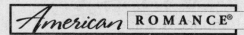

Heart, Home & Happiness!

YES! Please send me 2 FREE Harlequin American Romance® novels and my 2 FREE gifts. After receiving them, if I don't wish to receive any more books, I can return the shipping statement marked "cancel." If I don't cancel, I will receive 4 brand-new novels every month and be billed just $4.24 per book in the U.S., or $4.99 per book in Canada, plus 25¢ shipping and handling per book and applicable taxes, if any*. That's a savings of close to 15% off the cover price! I understand that accepting the 2 free books and gifts places me under no obligation to buy anything. I can always return a shipment and cancel at any time. Even if I never buy another book from Harlequin, the two free books and gifts are mine to keep forever.

154 HDN EEZK   354 HDN EEZV

Name	(PLEASE PRINT)	
Address		Apt. #
City	State/Prov.	Zip/Postal Code

Signature (if under 18, a parent or guardian must sign)

Mail to the Harlequin Reader Service®:
IN U.S.A.: P.O. Box 1867, Buffalo, NY 14240-1867
IN CANADA: P.O. Box 609, Fort Erie, Ontario L2A 5X3

Not valid to current Harlequin American Romance subscribers.

Want to try two free books from another line?
Call 1-800-873-8635 or visit www.morefreebooks.com.

* Terms and prices subject to change without notice. NY residents add applicable sales tax. Canadian residents will be charged applicable provincial taxes and GST. This offer is limited to one order per household. All orders subject to approval. Credit or debit balances in a customer's account(s) may be offset by any other outstanding balance owed by or to the customer. Please allow 4 to 6 weeks for delivery.

Your Privacy: Harlequin is committed to protecting your privacy. Our Privacy Policy is available online at www.eHarlequin.com or upon request from the Reader Service. From time to time we make our lists of customers available to reputable firms who may have a product or service of interest to you. If you would prefer we not share your name and address, please check here. ☐

HAR07

Inside ROMANCE

Stay up-to-date on all your romance reading news!

Inside Romance is a FREE quarterly newsletter highlighting our upcoming series releases and promotions.

Visit

www.eHarlequin.com/InsideRomance

to sign up to receive our complimentary newsletter today!

IRNL07

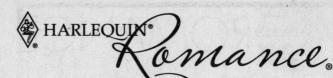

HARLEQUIN® Romance®

MEDITERRANEAN DADS

In the first of this emotional Mediterranean Dads duet,
nanny Julie is whisked away to a palatial Italian villa,
but she feels completely out of place in Massimo's
glamorous world. Her biggest challenge, though, is
ignoring her attraction to the brooding tycoon.

Look for

The Italian Tycoon
and the Nanny

by **Rebecca Winters**

in March wherever you buy books.

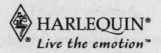

HARLEQUIN®
Live the emotion™

www.eHarlequin.com   HRI7500

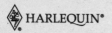

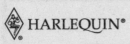

HARLEQUIN®

American ★ Romance®

COMING NEXT MONTH

#1201 THE GENTLEMAN RANCHER by Cathy Gillen Thacker
Texas Legacies: The Carrigans
When Taylor O'Quinn left Texas to pursue a writing career, Jeremy Carrigan missed his former best friend more than she'd ever know. Seeing her again makes him want more than just the camaraderie they used to share. Can he convince the now famous novelist to help a certain doctor-turned-gentleman-rancher stay put in Laramie—as Jeremy's friend, lover and wife?

#1202 GOIN' DOWN TO GEORGIA by Ann DeFee
Magnolia Bluffs, Georgia, looks like the perfect small Southern town. But big-city detective Zack Maynard smells trouble brewing below the surface with a real estate development his family has invested in. And that means dealing with one of the company partners, Liza Henderson, a not-so-perfect small Southern woman. Although, as Zack discovers, perfection is a quality that might be seriously overrated!

#1203 AN UNLIKELY MOMMY by Tanya Michaels
Fatherhood
After growing up with a trio of overprotective brothers, Ronnie Carter is ready to break loose and live a little. But she gets more than she bargained for when she meets handsome high school teacher Jason McDeere and his irresistible toddler daughter. Although Ronnie hadn't planned on taking on a ready-made family, Jason and Emily are rapidly turning the town mechanic's mind to motherhood…

#1204 THE PILOT'S WOMAN by Ann Roth
When D. J. Hatcher helps Liza Miller board his seaplane, it's déjà vu for both of them. Three years ago D.J. flew the jilted bride home. Now she's coming back to beautiful Halo Island—but is it to stay? Liza seems reluctant to start a relationship with a man who has also been burned by love. Do the sultry breezes and sizzling sunsets portend romance…and second chances?

HARCNM0208